Paper Kingdom

Other Stories

Celeste Young

Grosvenor House
Publishing Limited

This book is published by
Grosvenor House Publishing Ltd
Link House
140 The Broadway, Tolworth, Surrey, KT6 7HT.
www.grosvenorhousepublishing.co.uk

This book is a work of fiction. Any resemblance to
people or events, past or present, is purely coincidental.

A CIP record for this book
is available from the British Library

ISBN 978-1-80381-137-6

This book is dedicated to
David, Natasha, Stefan, and Tristan.

CONTENTS

PAPER KINGDOM

OTHER STORIES

PAPER KINGDOM

1

LAMENT FOR A CHINAMAN

Once upon a time, on a crisp spring morning, a Chinaman from the village of Hui Yin, left China and sailed west. He followed the Sun Star, carrying with him hunger, expectation, and fear, and eventually reached the savannahs of Africa. His womenfolk, left behind in the village, burned incense and paper money, and prayed to their ancestors for him to have a safe journey. Puffs of smoke spiralled in rings and wafted up towards the heavens, chiselling the air into a bony monkey, a plump cow, a bird, and then the bony monkey again. Sculpture of premonition and doom: the women began to wail. In the village temple, tonsured soothsayers chanted prophecies: "Chinaman, oh Chinaman, multiply and prosper, but Africa will never be yours, for it is written in the stars that…" The women's loud sobbing drowned the monotonous chanting.

… And it came to pass that four decades later, on a chilly winter evening in Africa, three generations of Chinamen fled west on the wings of a red and white steel bird. Nomads of survival, they were now flying from their African purgatory to the concrete jungle.

Ah, Man's unquenched thirst for Heaven!

2

ONE ENCHANTED EVENING

On my eighth birthday, we moved into our new house.

The first thing we children did was to run to the two bathrooms and open the bath taps. We tingled with excitement as hot and cold water splashed down on our cupped hands and tumbled warm into the bath. That evening, we each took two baths. Both bathrooms in our new house were large and alabaster-floored, with gleaming, white-tiled walls and a wide round window that gazed at a clear blue sky on sunny days. For me, they exuded prosperity against the memory of the unsheltered concrete backyard, mercilessly exposed to the open air all year round, where we had our baths in wooden tubs in the olden days. Mother used to scrub my brothers' feet hard and, boxing their ears, reprimanded them, saying: "You naughty boys, roaming around barefoot and playing in infested swamps. The Portuguese say that we Chinese are poor and dirty. Poor yes, but dirty, no!" And she spanked them.

There in the yard, our washed linen fluttered dry in the sun, and a cluster of chickens pecked at soggy burnt brown rice grains scraped from the bottom of a cooking pan, indifferent to the fate of their companions. My mother, crouched over the gutter, held a dangling chicken by its feathery throat, and with a quick movement of her right hand slit it open. A pool of blood coursed down the gutter, leaving the grid bright red. For us children, however gruesome the sight of the slaughter was, it nevertheless heralded the welcome treat of coconut and peanut chicken for dinner, the only local dish my parents had taken to instantly when they first arrived in the country. They improved on its original recipe by adding a Chinese touch to it, flavouring it with a good sprinkling of light soy sauce.

Yes, we used to live at the back of our shop in the Maquinino area of Beira, near the harbour and the railway station. Our square-shaped shop occupied the largest room in our one-storey terraced house with a corrugated iron roof, one in an endless row of house shops owned by an Indian landlord. He was, my father said, one of the descendants of a British Indian trader who settled along the Zambezi in the late nineteenth century. Nestling beside the shop was a long narrow room where my mother, my second brother Luís and I slept in a large bed, with a wooden flap that was pulled up at night. I used to hold my mother's little finger until I fell asleep, for the gentle pricking sensation of her smooth round nail digging into the flesh of my hand reassured me of her presence, and chased away my fear of the dark, when relatives' angry and vengeful spirits prowled around in the labyrinth of my nightmares. (Mother said that, many years ago, father's dead patron uncle claimed and took the lives of two of her children, as an act of punishment and revenge against their behaviour during his funeral service. When he died, my mother took her two children to the funeral, but as they were then very young, they didn't understand the solemnity of the occasion and, growing listless with the ceremony going on around them, they decided to play. They whispered and giggled. And when the time came for them to cast a handful of earth over the coffin, they instead kicked the surrounding sand over the gaping hole. In recurring nightmares, my mother dreamt and heard my father's uncle reprimand her for not bringing up her children properly, and to teach her a lesson, he added, he would take her two children away. She begged for clemency and forgiveness, but her plea was to no avail. A month later, the children went on a picnic to the beach with the Chinese School, and drowned in the vastness of the Indian Ocean.) In this same room slept my elder brother Carlos and second sister Clara, both in narrow single beds stacked against the bare wall. Countless other cousins slept here too, packed like sardines, on days when they travelled down to Beira from rural areas. And when the time came for them to start primary education at the local Chinese school, where both Portuguese and Chinese were taught, they came to live with us permanently.

At the far end of this dormitory was my eldest sister's bedroom, a tiny rectangle partitioned from our room by a thin brick wall. She was the only one in the house who had a corner of her own, and we children were instructed not to enter it without a formal invitation. Child trespassers who prowled outside the forbidden territory were reminded by my mother that "Sofia, sister number one, is a woman now. She needs privacy. Go and play outside." Sofia, who bore the name of the Greek midwife who had delivered her and subsequently became her godmother, had a wind-up phonograph, and it was this toy that riveted our curiosity and drew us into her room whenever she was out. In her private corner, where magazine cuttings of favourite film stars were glued all over the walls, she played her Crosbies, Sinatras, and Dean Martins endlessly.

Sofia had silky blue-black hair, large almond eyes, and a porcelain complexion – her striking features captured in a serene oval frame. She knew she was beautiful (people never tired of telling her so) and bore herself with style and a dramatic sense of destiny. In the privacy of her own room, she acted and lived out her fantasies, and we often caught her playing different roles in a Hollywood movie. The dream, the drive, and the expectations of becoming a film star were hers, but the opportunity never came. In fact, a sense of expectation hovered over our lives in Mozambique, but the object of that expectation always eluded us, leaving us with a vague feeling of transience and doom against the concrete permanence of underdevelopment and poverty, heat, dust, and mosquitoes.

My father suffered from acute asthma and, on the doctor's advice, slept alone in a minuscule room adjoining our shop and entered into through a small screen door. Mother got up very early in the mornings to bake crusty bread and make cakes to sell for the day. By the time I was up, the railway and port workers had already been into our shop to buy their breakfast, and my brothers and sisters had gone to school. I sat on a stool next to Mother, rolled tobacco to make cigarettes, and packed them neatly into a large tin. Our African customers, whose means were meagre, bought these cigarettes singly. Perched on a high stool, I helped Mother weigh sugar in brown paper bags on a bronze scale tinged with a soft green patina. And bearing my child's height firmly over low boxes, I dug a wooden cube measure into the maize flour and confidently filled up our customers' sacks. In the evenings, we children ate up pieces of unsold stale bread. We carved a deep hole in the hard flesh of the bread, filled it with sugar, and poured warm water into the well, making a soft, moist pudding.

That birthday evening, July 7th, was laden with magic. A diamond-studded indigo veil descended upon it, and a large silver disc, having slanted across the heavens and hovered past the vast region between the rivers Rovuma and Buzi, came to rest over Beira. The pulsating of the twinkling stars was in unison with the punctuated rhythm of the cicadas' hissing and the frogs' croaking. Silver butterflies, uncertain of their destination, fluttered over the weedy surface of the pond by our new house, and then flapped away to repose on the evergreen hedge. A pair of dragonflies, with gold-rimmed mother-of-pearl wings, glided forth and found a lovers' nest amid the pink petals of the prodigious water-lilies. A faint sound of beating drums and frenzied *batuque* wafted in from far away in the direction of Munhava.

Suddenly, in an abrupt crescendo, the loud boom of a gong pierced the unbroken night. The moon stirred from its slumber. And a myriad of images, reflections of a Chinaman's haunted imagination, flickered across the silver kaleidoscope, without which nourishment his exiled soul would perish in Africa, away from his homeland. Golden dragons hissed, spread their wings, and spat out blankets of *cacimbo* into the air. And rustling giant paper goldfishes with goggle eyes, swimming in different directions, blew the *cacimbo* across the chilly night.

The sound of the gong jerked me from my sleep. I opened my eyes only to find that familiar mosquito net draped over me. The solid metal fan hung reassuringly above my head. I went back to sleep.

Five celestial creatures with milk-glass complexions arrived at the Great River. One of them held a child by his hand, and another carried a baby on her back. Attired in mulberry satin quilted jackets, they mounted three snow-white feathery ducks. At first, the ducks paddled their feet to get a better balance, and then glided, ferrying their passengers across the sweet-wine river of libation. Incense sticks grew along the river's edge and an intoxicating scent permeated the air. When they reached the land of sleeping earthlings, the night travellers dismounted.

At a quarter to midnight, our guard-dog whined. My parents, who now slept in the same room, my father having been cured of his asthma, heard the entrance door to our new house slam shut and footsteps of laughing, chattering youths skip lightly up the stairs and make for the dining-room. The youths opened the large fridge standing in a corner of the dining-room, inspected the food left over from our house-warming party, and helped themselves to some chopped steamed chicken dipped in oyster sauce. They opened bottles of coke, threw the tops into the air, and licked the sizzling froth surfing down their fingers. A shower of bottle tops clattered against the polished wooden floor. Having had their fill, they set out to look for my parents. They filed past several bedrooms down the long narrow corridors, and their light footsteps stopped outside my parents' room. And in the curtained darkness, my parents made out the silhouettes of the five children they had lost, standing in a ring right in the middle of their room. They giggled among themselves and in a tuneful chorus sang out: "Mother and Father, you have such a nice house and such nice food!" Warm tears sprang from my father's eyes, tumbled down his frozen, hollow cheeks, and fell like white jade drops into his hands. My mother reached out for the night visitors, trying to touch them. "We will be back again. We will come and visit you," chanted the voices. The shadows vanished. Choked by mixed emotions, my father whispered, "If only these children could share with their brothers and sisters the good fortune that came so late in our lives...", and he sank back into his bed. My mother covered him with a blanket and said, "But they do, husband, in their own way."

At breakfast the next morning, my mother regaled us with the story of my dead siblings' visit. "And they drank and ate the leftovers from our supper, too," she added. Incredulous, I ran to look in the fridge and pointed out that both the food and bottles of coke remained intact from the previous night. "Yes," my brother Luís said, "if they did in fact come back to feast on our food and drink, how come everything looks intact, just as we left it last night before we went to bed?"

"Ah!" my mother retorted, with a slight tone of censure in her voice, "it is the spirit of the food and coke they ate and drank last night. And to understand this mystery, you have to be Chinese." And she repeated, "Chinese."

My mother's observation that morning haunted my imagination until I reached adulthood. I have not forgotten that enchanted birthday evening nor the jade drops on creased yellow silk. As time condensed the memories and images of my childhood and youth into my cosmic essence, the complex poetry of being Chinese and Mozambican gradually matured into something simple and yet profound.

3

THE NIGHT OF
THE GREEN LIGHT

On the heat-soaked evenings, the dormitory in our old house baked like an oven. My family sat out on the concrete pavement outside our shop, and waited for the night to cool before going indoors to sleep. Often, our Chinese neighbours and friends joined us. Adults brought folding chairs, and children empty slatted wooden soap crates to sit on. We burned incense rings to keep the mosquitoes away. Grown-ups gossiped over daily events, and children played games on the dust road. To while away the hours, my parents took their turn to story-tell about life and relatives back in China, and the reasons why they had emigrated to Africa.

When I search for moments of my past, thoughts of jade pursue me insistently. For although I was born in Mozambique, China is my childhood and adolescence. And the China of my childhood is not one of great works of art or revolutionary heroes, or the Long March. It is a China of deprivation and emigration, superstition and magical symbolism.

One sweaty evening, two days before the lunar New Year, we sat out as usual. The whole of Machado dos Santos Street, where we lived, was keeping vigil on our next-door neighbour, Mr Babu. We called him Mr Babu because he was Indian, and we Chinese children called every Indian man Mr Babu. Our Babu had been ill for some time, but the precise nature of his illness was never mentioned in the presence of children. Adults hinted at it in whispers laden with shame. They said that Babu would not see the New Year in, and a doctor and a nurse had been toing and froing from his shop that whole afternoon. Babu was a tailor. He had bolts of colourful cotton cloths, which inexplicably attracted African women of all sizes and shapes into his shop. Cloths with similar patterns were passed unnoticed and unpurchased in the other shops of our neighbourhood. He was a confirmed bachelor, and kept a buxom *mulata* assistant. We children eavesdropped on a rumour that his assistant was not keeping his bed warm enough, and that explained why other women customers left Babu's shop with meters and meters of cloth, free of charge. As we greeted Babu each morning, we children noticed that his face looked yellower and yellower, and marked with sores. Sharp, feline tongues wagged that Babu's women customers were transmitting their poison into his blood, and although we children did not quite understand the euphemism, we could tell that Babu was very ill.

My mother said that in her China, you had to watch out for two colours of light – red and green – if you fell gravely ill and your life hung by a thread. A red light meant you were not ready to cross the Great River, and you would therefore recover from your illness in due course. A green light, on the other hand, signalled death, and your ancestors would therefore make the necessary preparations to receive you in the other world.

As we awaited news of Babu's deteriorating condition, we looked out for any significant hues of red or green that might point to Babu's fate that night. But the hours crawled by, and no news of change in Babu's condition! I played hop-scotch on the pavement. But on the stroke of ten, I asked my mother on a whim to tell us a story, and sat on a soap crate by her feet. She began to story-tell.

Once upon a time, in the village of Hui Yin, in Southern China, there lived a young man called Diligent. He lived with his widowed mother and three younger brothers. They were poor peasants and tilled their small farm from dawn to sunset. Life was hard, and what their land yielded was just enough to keep them fed and alive from year to year. They feared typhoons, especially strong and multiple ones, which caused floods and destroyed crops and made people homeless. Diligent's mother raised chickens, ducks, and pigs, which her sons sold in the neighbouring market town. They themselves ate meat only on very special occasions, such as the New Year and birthdays.

Diligent was only fourteen when his father died. A boy made man long before his time. Bequeathed with the onerous task of leading a family at such a tender age, he nevertheless bore his new responsibility with as much imagination and dignity as a responsible teenager could muster. But many a time, he begrudged the fate the gods had bestowed on him and, bewildered, he retreated to the shade of the weeping willow by the narrow river which meandered through his village. There, in the solitude, he tried to sort out his pained thoughts and feelings. He wanted to grow up an educated man, become a scholar, and earn decent wages in the city. He didn't want to be a peasant farmer for the rest of his days. But he also remembered his mother's words on the day of the funeral. She had said, "Diligent, my son, you are the eldest of my boys, you are now the head of this family." With these words in mind, Diligent held back his tears and returned to the farm, determined to cope with his predicament.

The following year, the harvest was bad, and there was no longer enough food to feed the impoverished household. Diligent's mother then decided to sell her youngest son, Knight, to a childless couple, who were also distant relatives of hers. After Knight had left to live in a neighbouring village, his meagre belongings bundled in a white cotton sheet tied in a knot, Diligent cried like a baby for several weeks. "It isn't strictly speaking a sale," his mother consoled him, "it is a loan! When Knight is older and life gets better here, we will buy him back. My relatives are childless and will treat your brother well, not like a slave. You will see how everything will work out well." At fifteen, Diligent felt fatherless, while now also playing the role of a husband.

Diligent had been a bright, intelligent, and hard-working pupil at the village school. Although he still harboured dreams of going to university in his heart, he now banished them from his mind. A sagacious youth, he was conscious of the need to acquire some practical skill to supplement the family income. Moved by Diligent's luckless fate, his village school teacher offered to continue tutoring him in his spare time. With him, Diligent learned the basics of book-keeping, and in due course found a part-time job as an accountant to a small trader in a town near his village. He went on farming the family land alongside his two brothers, but his heart was no longer in the land.

When Diligent was nineteen, his brother Knight was reunited with the family. His adoptive parents found him an extremely difficult youth to live with, "a loafer and a good-for-nothing," they called him; and as Diligent was now earning a supplementary income, he negotiated the re-purchase of his lost brother. Knight was happy to be home again, but deep in his heart the resentment against his own brothers and mother began to infest him. He hated his mother for having selected him to be sold, and avenged himself by being boorish and uncooperative in the house and unhelpful on the farm. Guilt-ridden, his brothers and mother couldn't bring themselves to coerce Knight into behaving otherwise. Knight continued living as a parasite and a loafer, and even when he became a father, never acquired a sense of responsibility.

Soon after Diligent's twenty-first birthday, his mother said, "My son, you are now a man and must have a wife. An extra pair of hands will be a great help in the house, and a daughter-in-law would make a comforting companion for me while you and your brothers are out in the fields. I am getting older and older, and am beginning to feel in my bones the end of my days." So Diligent's mother sent for the village matchmaker and advertised her search for a daughter-in-law. The requirements for the position were basic and simple. She would be young, healthy, and strong, hardworking, obedient, and respectful of her elders. "I have just the right candidate for you," said the go-between, remembering an eighteen-year-old girl called Beautiful Clothes, the unassuming and uncomplaining daughter of an equally humble peasant family in the next village.

The matchmaker arranged for the two families concerned to meet and discuss the preliminaries for a possible marriage between Diligent and Beautiful Clothes. And on the fixed date, one hot morning in summer, Diligent and Beautiful Clothes met for the first time. Mother and son sat at a creaky round table in a bare room, sipped tea, and exchanged banal pleasantries with Beautiful Clothes and her parents. Beautiful Clothes, glancing shyly at her suitor, wondered why Diligent, being Chinese like herself, had such a dark complexion, and even thought he looked more Indian than Chinese. Although Diligent was born a peasant, his aristocratic-looking hooked nose, complemented by a glowing olive complexion and large almond eyes, gave him the countenance of a prince, Beautiful Clothes thought. An Aztec prince, she called Diligent many, many years later. And after three rounds of sweet-scented tea, both parties liked each other enough to approve of the arranged marriage, and settled there and then a date for the wedding, and bargained for the family wedding gifts. As soon as Diligent left, Beautiful Clothes's father said to his daughter, "Mark me, that nose is a rich man's nose. One day, my daughter, your betrothed will be a rich man." His wife nodded in agreement.

In her new home, Beautiful Clothes worked very hard, and although her mother-in-law was not unkind to her, her brothers-in-law who still lived in the same house bullied her constantly, especially Knight. Within the first year of her marriage, Beautiful Clothes gave birth to a son, who died of polio soon afterwards. Barely recovering from the grief of their personal loss, Diligent and Beautiful Clothes were soon afflicted by another devastating loss. One unforgettable year, protracted cycles of monsoons struck the village and destroyed all the crops. Diligent's family was made homeless and had to rebuild and farm from scratch. At this point in time, Diligent began to talk of emigrating, of trying his luck in a new country. "When I have earned the fare for each of you to join me, I will send for you," he told his wife, mother, and brothers. But it wasn't until 1933 that Diligent, now thirty years old, left China and set out west for the dark land where an uncle of his had settled. Beautiful Clothes had just given birth to twin baby girls.

In 1887, a great-uncle of Diligent's was contracted, among many young Cantonese workers, by the Portuguese government to work in the building of railways in the southern regions of its African colony, Mozambique. When the railway link between Lourenço Marques and Transvaal was completed, Diligent's great-uncle, like many of his fellow countrymen, did not return to China. He settled in Mozambique, bought a small plot of land in the fertile valley of the River Pungue, became a market gardener, and sent for his wife and son. They joined him years later. His son, Diligent's uncle, took over the *machamba* when the old man passed away. On the fertile land, both father and son grew cash crops and Chinese vegetables, and lived a quiet and modest life, without the constant threat of monsoons. Diligent's uncle wrote to his relatives back in China from time to time, remained a bachelor, and seemed content to live in Mozambique.

When, on a crisp spring morning, Diligent left China, he had only a brown cardboard suitcase, a few Hong Kong dollars in his pocket, and a knot in his heart. His womenfolk, left behind in the village, burnt incense and paper money and prayed to their ancestors for a safe journey. Puffs of smoke spiralled in rings and lifted up towards the heavens, chiselling the air into a bony monkey, a plump cow, a bird, and then the bony monkey again. In the village temple, tonsured soothsayers chanted prophecies.

Diligent earned his one-way fare to Africa by enlisting as a sailor and working as a carpenter on a Japanese freighter. Once in Mozambique, he had to live by his wits. During the harvest season, he was trucked up to his uncle's *machamba* to work as a farmhand. At other times, he did odd jobs in Beira, helping as a carpenter or as an assistant to Mr Chin, who had a little shop in the African shanty town of Chipangara. He found lodgings in a large wooden house on stilts, owned by the local Association of Chinese Residents, and paid a small rent for a tiny square room. There, he enjoyed the companionship of fellow residents, young men like himself who had gone to Africa to try their luck, and made lasting friendships with two of them, Mr Yan and Mr Lo, without which he would have been unbearably homesick. With the small savings he had made, Diligent bought a licence and some merchandise, and became a street vendor. He sold basic food items, such as rice, maize flour, dried shrimps, and salted fish. He pedalled his cart to work, along flat sun-baked dust roads, beads of sweat gleaming on his high forehead. By the time his mother passed away in China, Diligent had saved enough to send for his wife, who arrived in Beira after a long and turbulent sea journey on a third-class passenger ticket. Diligent approached his uncle for a loan to help open a shop of his own, and as Beautiful Clothes was now in the new land as Diligent's work partner, his uncle dutifully obliged. The reunited couple rented a shop house in the area of Maquinino. And there, they made their home.

My mother paused and, patting my hand with affection, added, "And this, Estrela, is where your father and I started our lives here in Beira." She was about to resume her story, but seeing that my concentration had wandered, she smiled and said, "I see you don't want to hear more stories. You want to play now. Go then." I clambered to my feet and waddled a few steps to where a concrete pillar supported the pavement arcade, and where I had placed my rubber ball. I bounced the ball and threw it against the front wall of our shop several times. "Mind you don't smash the shop window, Estrela," my mother said, in a resigned voice.

Suddenly, I caught sight of a prick of green light fall from the sky. It became a large green jade ball and rolled in the direction of Babu's shop. My mother shouted, "Everybody indoors, and don't look back." We shuffled our feet under the weight of scraping chairs and stampeded back into the house. I could not resist the temptation of looking back over my shoulder. And because I was too cowardly to turn round and stare straight at the green light, I peered from the corner of my eye. I saw a large disc of jade dust whirl anti-clockwise around a solid jade heart. When it reached Babu's door, the dust dispersed and dissolved into the dark night. The sparkling green heart wobbled by the door, squeezed itself under it, and rolled into Babu's shop, casting an incandescent green glow on the whole house.

Early next morning, an ambulance arrived and took Babu away. He was dead.

On the same morning, a dead body was discovered floating in the mosquito and excrement-infested waters of the muddy river which cut across Maquinino. It was Mr Fung's body. Mr Fung was also a neighbour and lived fourteen doors away from ours. It was rumoured that he had committed suicide, a caged animal tortured to death by his own sense of sexual inadequacy. Although I was only a child at the time, adult sneers gave me to understand that Mrs Fung was a loose woman. She was ostracised by her own community as a disgrace to her race, because she allowed herself to be frequented and abused by Portuguese men. For although the Chinese coexisted with settlers of other races, in the 1950s they rarely crossed the racial divide, and despised any of their women who did in matters of courtship and marriage. Or plain whoring. And even a decade and a half later, when a trickle of self-confident and educated Chinese Mozambicans began to marry people of other races, such unions were tolerated and accepted as a fait accompli rather than approved.

On the night of the green light, while all eyes and ears were on Babu's imminent departure from this world, a tragic drama was unfolding at number 124, unnoticed by outsiders. Mr Fung, a fireman on the railways, arrived home from his evening shift an hour earlier than his wife expected. He found Mrs Fung in bed with a Portuguese stranger. Fuming with rage, he grabbed an empty beer bottle standing on a low table, cracked it on the bedroom wall, and moved menacingly towards his wife, ignoring her Portuguese companion who fled naked from the house. Mrs Fung remained in bed, paralysed by fear, and clutched the sheets helplessly under her chin. Mr Fung flung the sheets away from her slim, milky body, and tearing apart her silky legs, he pushed the broken bottle neck up into her vagina.

"You filthy whore! You disgust me with your lechery," he spat at her.

"And you disgust me with your whining," she retaliated, spelling out every word with calm and quiet, in spite of her physical pain, deliberately hurting his macho pride. Roaring like a wounded animal, he beat her hard until he was breathless. Repulsed by his own violence, and ashamed of the cruelty he had just unleashed on his wife, Mr Fung ran wild into the night.

Mrs Fung felt the sharp edges of the cold glass cut and tear through the dark intimate parts of her innerself. Bleeding and trembling with pain, she felt her body explode and glass fragments shoot out through her pores, sprinkling the night misty white with its powder. She screamed for help, and her anguished cry split open the universe. Amid the chaos, she saw a luminous red parachute drop slowly from the night sky. As it floated down towards her, the parachutist's face become more identifiable. It bore features of a beautiful Eurasian child with penetrating dark almond eyes. She landed, took off her flying helmet and shook her hazelnut brown hair, staring deeply and meaningfully into Mrs Fung's eyes. Mrs Fung felt a sense of timelessness soothe her pained body. As silently and mysteriously as she had descended, the child walked away into the night. Inside Mrs Fung's throbbing head, stars flashed out a prophecy she could not understand. She imagined she read something along the lines of: "Woman, the fruit of your womb will make history. Rejoice!" Mrs Fung did not dare to mention it, in case people thought she had dreams of greatness to add to the ugly names they had already heaped on her. Crawling along the concrete floor, she dragged her bruised body to her front door, and cried out for help. Her next-door neighbour who in normal circumstances would have ignored her, took pity on this occasion, and cycled to the public hospital to get help. Charitable Franciscan nuns nursed Mrs Fung back to health and took her in as a resident in the orphanage run by the Order. One rain-washed morning, when the white bougainvillea was in full bloom, Mrs Fung gave birth to a beautiful, healthy girl.

4

A HOUSE FOR A PATRIARCH

In 1952, there was only one Chinese architect in Beira, and his name was Mr Long. No-one knew exactly where he had got his professional qualifications, and no one made a point of querying them. What mattered was that his skills were seen to work in practice. But it was rumoured that Mr Long had never graduated as an architect in China, and that he bought his diploma in Macao.

My father had faith in Mr Long as an architect, and sent him a formal invitation to call at the house. Mr Long was elated. Six months earlier, he had asked for my father's permission to marry my sister Sofia through a go-between, but my father purred and demurred without rejecting or accepting his proposal. Now, Mr Long reasoned, a personal invitation from my father meant only one thing: a formal approval, for a rejection from my father would have been conveyed to him through the go-between. He put on a cream-coloured linen suit and white pointed shoes, grinned at the mirror, and vaselined his hair neatly. Rubbing his hands with self-satisfaction and humming to himself, he left his bachelor flat in Chinatown and headed for Maquinino.

It was a Saturday afternoon, and all the shops were closed. When Mr Long arrived at my house, my father met him in the shop and shook hands with him warmly. The two men exchanged formal greetings, and Mr Long's narrow eyes glinted, while his bloated cheeks flushed in great expectation. He was about to begin a speech, which he had been rehearsing since he received the invitation, but checked himself when he saw my mother come into the shop with a tray containing a teapot and two cups, and place it on the counter. Mr Long rose from his chair and greeted my mother profusely, kow-towing several times. My mother said that she hoped Mr Long would enjoy his visit and the tea, and then bade him farewell, leaving the two men to discuss business.

"Mr Long, I've sent for you because I want to commission you to design a house for me," announced my father.

Mr Long couldn't believe his ears. He was so disappointed that his facial features dropped as if they had been pulled down by the force of gravity. He stammered, saying, "But I thought you had sent for me to discuss my proposal of marriage to your daughter."

"Oh, that! There is plenty of time for us to think about that. My daughter is only nineteen. First, we must talk business. Later on, in the course of time, we'll talk about personal matters. I could have hired a Portuguese architect, but no, I want to confer on you the honour of designing my first home in this country. If I didn't hold you in such high esteem, I wouldn't have selected you as the architect of the house I propose to build."

Mr Long was flattered. Timidly, he ventured to say, "I will design for you a house you can be proud of. But I ask you again to bear in mind my marriage proposal, and give me a definite answer when I've finished designing your house. This is a fair request, isn't it? I am pushing thirty-five and would like to get married."

"Well said, Mr Long. Let us drink to your future and my house!" My father poured the jasmine tea into the cups and offered one to Mr Long. Then the two men raised their cups and proposed a toast: "To the house! To the future!" My father and Mr Long slurped the warm liquid with the gusto of men who set out to celebrate their peasant origins.

"And what kind of house do you have in mind?" Mr Long asked.

At this question, my father smiled openly, one of those rare smiles that made him look rejuvenated and light-hearted. Otherwise, he usually looked pensive and serious. He leaned slowly against the back of his chair and said, his eyes glistening, "I am thinking of a house that is large enough to accommodate my current family, that of my two sons and that of my male grandchildren. My three daughters will get married one day and leave my household to go and live with their husbands' families. But my two sons and their families will live with me and my wife. And I shall rule over them, guard their welfare, and guide them in my old age with wisdom and foresight. I want a house in a circular shape, with round windows, to commemorate that historic moment in my life when I looked out of a porthole on the Japanese freighter I was in, and glimpsed the silver-sanded, pine-lined beaches of Beira as we neared land. I knew then that I had arrived at my destination. You, Mr Long, have a free hand in the design itself. I must specify that I want a large communal sitting-room and dining-room for my sons' families, but a separate kitchen and bathroom for each. I also want a roof garden as a gift to my wife, who is a keen gardener. I plan to let the ground-floor of the building as offices or commercial premises. I calculate that the income from the ground-floor rents will pay for the maintenance and upkeep of my future home."

After a lengthy discussion over details, my father and Mr Long parted company. My father reached for his abacus and flicked the black beads, doing more sums and noting them down on a piece of paper. He folded and pocketed his note, and went back to his room with the abacus. From the window of his tiny room, he could see my mother in the steam-filled kitchen making dumplings for my brother Luís's birthday party. My mother called out from the kitchen to no-one in particular and asked for the time. My sister Sofia shouted three o'clock from her quarters. Soon, Luís's friends would be arriving.

"I have come some way now," my father reflected, "and the house I'm going to build for my family now will be the first of many to come." He opened the turquoise-coloured safe, took out some notes, and sealed them in a red envelope as a birthday present for Luís. He was about to lock the safe when he suddenly felt dizzy and groped for his chair. It stood a few steps away. The afternoon heat was humid and suffocating. The blurred sight of the actual money in the open coffers stirred in him memories of dark and violent moments way back, when he used to chase luck and seek solace in seedy gambling houses. When he regained his composure, he felt calmer and mentally addressed his thoughts to my mother as he watched her from his window.

"I often wonder whether you've really forgiven me for what I did to you and Estrela that evening when I returned home late, coughing my lungs out. I know I shouldn't have gone out that night, because the *cacimbo* was so thick and damp. But no *cacimbo* on earth would have stopped me from going out to gamble in those days. I had just lost all my cash at the gambling table and was in utter despair. When I arrived home, you were still up, and in the shop getting things ready for the following day, and our infant daughter was sitting on that blue potty of hers. I asked you whether you had washed her and whether she was ready for bed. You told me you hadn't had time."

"What, the toddler isn't ready for bed yet? Do you realise what the fucking time is, you bitch?" I swore at you.

"And who are you to talk about time?" You replied so defiantly.

My frustration boiled over. I pounced on you in a frenzy, and I hit you again and again until you bled. And then Estrela got up from her potty, crying and screaming, and ran to me, trying to kick me. I grabbed her and hurled her through the air, and I still remember that thump as she fell to the floor in the far corner of the room. Then the other children, who were asleep, woke up with the noise and rushed into the shop. I remember you cursed me through all that blood gushing from your mouth, and you picked Estrela up in your arms and you tugged her ears gently, chanting: "Fear no fear, fear no fear," like a monk. Our children said nothing, but I could read their hatred and contempt in the way they stared at me. I felt so ashamed of myself then. And yes, although Estrela was still so tiny, I don't think she has ever forgiven me either. She is, and always will be, your girl.

"My asthma plagued me at the best of times, but after that, I almost died of pneumonia. I spent the next two months confined to bed, my life hanging by a thread. You worked in the shop single-handed, and you nursed this invalid in a spirit that seemed to suggest you had forgiven me, at least outwardly. But it was your unflagging stamina and courage at that time which challenged me into taking stock of myself, and proved a turning-point in my life. I vowed to turn over a new leaf and never to gamble again, if I survived my illness. Instead, I would work my guts out and be smart enough to get on in life. That's when our fortunes began to rise. That licence I won for importing and exporting goods meant I could rent a warehouse right here in Maquinino, and expand into wholesaling. And I haven't looked back. Business has been good, and my bank manager has confidence in me, so much so that he has agreed to give me a loan to build a house of my own. We will leave this hovel as soon as our new house is built. I promise you."

My father's house – a patriarch's house – took a year and a half to materialise, from the time of its conception to the time of its completion. It was very large and spacious, and had ten bedrooms. The outside of the house was painted yellow. It became known as the *Casa Girassol*, because an aerial view of the house, with its spherical shape and a roof garden spilling over with a profusion of flowers and plants, reminded the viewer of a sunflower. And apart from my immediate family, it housed countless relatives who had come to live with us over the years. Uncle Knight's four children, Uncle Jovial's four children, and Uncle Phoenix's three children, were all brought up in the patriarch's house. When my brothers got married and grandchildren were born, the latter were raised here under their grandfather's domineering wings. For in his house, the patriarch reigned supreme with a rod of iron.

From the front veranda of the house, I, at the age of eight and in the company of Chinese relatives and friends, innocently waved a Portuguese flag, clapping and shouting "Viva Portugal", as the President of the Portuguese Republic, Craveiro Lopes, and his motorcade passed our house. Looking handsome and lean in his white uniform, he looked up and, smiling graciously, waved back at us. At that particular moment, the transistor in the house was announcing that the

President had come to the province of Mozambique to bring greetings to all his people and reassure us that the black, brown, yellow, and white-skinned inhabitants were all Portuguese. But ours was a multi-racist society, although the Portuguese posture on race issues had always boasted of a history of non-racial discrimination or prejudice.

On top of the social pyramid sat the Portuguese with his paunch, his love of wine, and his lust for native women; and while he looked down on the yellows, the browns, and the blacks, these as individual groups looked down on one another in turn. The Chinese felt superior to the Indians and the Black Africans, and the Indians felt superior to the Chinese and the Blacks. The Goans, regardless of how others viewed them, felt and behaved more like the Portuguese than the Portuguese themselves. All these groups considered the Black Africans inferior, regarding them as no more than providers of cheap labour. Traders despised them, while at the same time seeking their custom. If the Africans hated their Portuguese masters for having conquered and colonised them, they resented and despised the Chinese and Indians even more, for the Asians were neither white nor black, and yet enjoyed the same privileges as the whites because of their economic self-sufficiency and independence. At best, the Chinese were looked upon as honorary whites who were obliged to their Portuguese ruler for giving them an opportunity to make a living in his colony, and buy land and property. My father, for one, considered himself lucky because, as he often reminded his children, his Chinese counterparts in neighbouring South Africa were not allowed to purchase land and property in white areas, in his time. And in spite of the apparent bonhomie of the Portuguese, the Chinese population knew and remembered its place in colonial society. As outsiders, because they were neither white nor black, and as rivals in a market which traded mainly with the native population, the Chinese and Indians understood one another, and as a result, held between them an unspoken bond of solidarity against the Portuguese or Africans, should the need arise.

My father had been right to trust Mr Long as an able architect. Today, in the eighties, the house that Mr Long designed and built for a patriarch still stands, strong and solid, undisturbed by the winds of change. It no longer stands as a monument to a self-made Chinese patriarch, but as a practical symbol of what an African patriarch's vision of socialism embraces in Mozambique. When we left in 1975, our house became state property.

As for Mr Long, well, he didn't get his coveted prize. My beautiful sister married a self-taught musician. And she married for love.

After we moved into the *Casa Girassol*, my father bought more plots of land and built more houses, offices, and commercial premises for letting. And as the city expanded by leaps and bounds, a cycle of investment, profit, and reinvestment, consolidated the patriarch's financial position. When my father went to the *Banco Nacional Ultramarino* to negotiate for loans to carry out his projects, the bank manager would tease my father, calling him "our African Mandarin". For in the Mozambican context, he had prospered and become a man of property. He was now a highly respected member of his community, one who was elected and re-elected for three consecutive terms of office as chairman of the Association of Chinese Residents. During that decade, he won as many admirers as enemies. The Portuguese colonists who envied and resented his newly-earned prosperity, tolerated it, nevertheless, in view of his contribution to the city's development. For this African mandarin, they said, invested and concentrated all his resources within the country, unlike some Chinese settlers whom they accused of diverting most of their wealth to other places, such as Hong Kong or Macao.

In the late Sixties and early Seventies, when his sons took over the family's import and export firm and business became stagnant, the patriarch was relieved at being able to fall back on his income from rents from his various properties to support his large, extended family. Many a time, the patriarch was faced with the threat of seeing his own firm swallowed up by greedy giant companies, but each time, with patience and calm confidence, he kept howling wolves from his door and resisted bowing to the short-term necessity of selling out.

5

A BIRTHDAY CELEBRATION

In September 1958, my mother gave a big party to celebrate my father's fifty-fifth birthday, and his silver jubilee in Mozambique. Relatives and friends of the family, as well as business acquaintances, were invited.

At the first crow of the cock, my mother and aunts, who had stayed in our house the night before, got up to set things ready for the day's festivities. The kitchen was a cascade of noise. And after a substantial breakfast of dumplings, coffee, and golden papaya, each of the women set out to prepare her own speciality. For they had come to cook for the patriarch's birthday lunch, as an expression of gratitude for what he had done for their families. Collectively, they put on a display of family unity and bonhomie, but underneath the ritualised domestic harmony, the ants were eating the women's souls away. For the venom of envy and jealousy, resentment and malice towards the patriarch's wife, entered their blood on the day the patriarch's house came into existence.

My aunt, Peach Blossom, Uncle Knight's wife, led the pack of hyenas. She and her brother ran a bar with an adjoining sweet shop. Her husband never worked, and spent his days at the Chinese Club or loafed around town, dropping in casually at his friends' shops for a good gossip. But promptly at four o'clock in the afternoon, he would get back to his own shop and sit by the entrance door to watch a Portuguese woman by the name of Clarisse pass along the street on her way home from work. She wasn't a beautiful woman, but she walked with her proud shoulders flung back, projecting the full weight of her overabundant breasts in a low-cut dress. Men wolf whistled at her in a chorus, and Uncle Knight sighed aloud, "Look at the Himalayas." After his daily titillation, he retreated to the Club for a game of mah-jong or poker, and returned home only at night.

Aunt Peach Blossom resented my mother for living in a large house of her own, while she and her husband and brother shared a small, rented flat. Her own children chose to live with us, because the patriarch had suggested that his house was big enough to accommodate them. And as they grew up, they showed no sign of wanting to return home to live with their mother. Nor was there any indication that Uncle Knight's prospects would improve during her lifetime. Peach Blossom hated the patriarch's wife for affording to be generous, warm, and conciliatory towards her, in spite of her bitchiness. In private conversations with her children, she advised them to eat their aunt out of house and home, and when her eldest son, Ferryboat, reached the age to get a driving licence, she urged him to crash his uncle's cars. And as she watched my mother grow fuller and rounder over the years, Peach Blossom thought she had at last found the weapon with which to hurt the patriarch's wife. She began to address my mother as "you, the fat aunt", in public. My mother, however, merely replied, unruffled: "Yes, Peach Blossom, I like a round body. It is a symbol of wholeness. Whereas a thin, flat body like yours stands for meanness. It is like a dried-up well."

If on my father's fifty-fifth birthday Peach Blossom only felt ants gnawing at her heart, years later, on her sick bed, she clasped my mother's hands in pain and cried, "I can't bear it any more. The ants are walking all over my body and eating my flesh away!" She was dying of cancer.

From mid-morning onwards, a string of relatives began to arrive for the repetitive ritual of exchanging gifts. Each family brought a large wooden tray of Portuguese and Chinese cakes. Neat rows of *pastéis de nata*, cream-filled pastry trumpets, and *bolos de arroz* sat next to dumplings, *woo kok*, and sesame buns. My mother took a dozen and a half of each variety from the tray, and left half a dozen for the family who brought the gift to take home. She untied the cramped legs of two live chickens brought to the house in a wicker basket, lifted one out and, carefully tying back the legs of the remaining chicken, left it lying uncomfortably in the basket. She opened the crate containing fat red plums, and handling them with gentleness, placed them in a glass bowl, leaving half a dozen in the wooden crate. And from a pile of boxes of birds' nests, Chinese sweets, and almond biscuits, she took one box of each, leaving the rest on the tray. To finalise the ritual, she gracefully slipped a thick red envelope under one of the boxes on the tray.

Nudging my mother, I whispered, "But, Mother, what is the red envelope for? It is Father's birthday. We shouldn't be the ones giving out presents!" Chuckling, my mother answered, "It is to pad out the tray, Estrela." And then she proceeded to repeat the same ritual with the next relative who came to the house bearing similar gifts.

By noon, the house was filled to bursting point, as each guest brought along at least eight members of his family. Children darted around playing, whilst adults grouped into clusters of conspiring minds. The guests who arrived early monopolised the air-conditioned sitting-room, but the more adventurous ones chose to go to the roof-garden. My parents milled around together in the crowd, shaking hands and exchanging greetings with the guests. When my father ran into Sofia, he asked, "Has Uncle Syrup gone to fetch Carlos from the airport?"

"Yes, about two hours ago," my sister said, "and they should be back by now. Should I send someone to check that Uncle Syrup isn't stuck somewhere with a flat tyre? You know what a clumsy driver he is. We've already phoned the airport. Carlos's flight was on time."

"We'll give him another half an hour. If they haven't arrived by then, we should perhaps send someone to find out what has happened."

My brother Carlos was studying in the capital city, Lourenço Marques, and was coming home for the weekend for my father's birthday party. I had been counting the days to see him home again, and now I was counting the minutes as I watched from a window for any sign of our Peugeot arriving. As a growing adolescent, I enjoyed going out to parties with my adult brother, and to partner him in grown-up dances like the tango, the cha-cha, and the rumba, while girls of his age, whose mothers eyed my brother as a good catch for their daughters, watched my well-coordinated steps on the dance floor with some irritation. And when my brother's friends called at the house, I showed off unashamedly and was flattered by the way they flirted with me. "Wait till you are twenty and I will marry you," they teased me, while I knew perfectly well that their attention and interest were totally riveted on my beautiful sister, Sofia. And when Sofia's male friends visited her, I proved such a nuisance that they had to bribe me in order to get rid of me. As the ice cream cart trilled its bell down our road, the visitors rushed out to buy me a cone of locally-made ice cream, after which I retired temporarily to my own room, only to re-emerge after a while in the sitting-room to torment them once more with my dreaded prattle and showing off.

A gleaming yellow dot appeared in the landscape. It grew larger and larger, until I could make out the shape of our car lurching round the flower-speckled roundabout, two hundred yards away from our house. I ran down the stairs, two steps at a time, to meet my brother. I was already standing on the pavement outside our house when Uncle Syrup drew the car to a halt and hooted, announcing my brother's arrival to the family. My brother flung open the front passenger door, leapt out, and threw his arms around me. "Oh, it's so good to have you home," I said, excited. To which he replied in a solemn tone, "It's good to be home," and he pecked me on the chin affectionately. He looked sad and apprehensive, and I couldn't imagine why he had so much luggage with him, as he was only expected home for the weekend.

Two of our African servants carried the suitcases into the house.

My brother was doing a course in Law and Economics in the capital, and my father hoped he would further his studies at the University of Lisbon later on. In fact, my father had always cherished the dream of sending each of his children back to China to study at the University of Peking when we reached higher education. It was a dream he, as a Chinaman, held for sentimental reasons and a vague sense of patriotism, without ever asking himself whether his children were expected to return to Mozambique or remain in China after the completion of their university studies. Subconsciously, he was trying to re-live, through us, a dream he had had to abandon many years back. But in his heart of hearts, my father knew that his children were not like him. They were born and raised in Mozambique; they were Chinese and Mozambican, but above all they were Mozambican. The revolution in China and Mao's triumphant inauguration of a Communist China in 1949 finally resolved my father's dilemma. Fundamentally anti-Communist, he became finally resigned to the idea of his children being educated outside China. But he retained his stubborn belief that Chang Kai-Shek's Nationalist Party would one day get mainland China back and free her from Communism.

Carlos was packed off to study in Lourenço Marques under the watchful eye of an uncle who lived in the capital city, and who briefed my father on every unsavoury move my brother made. A clipping from a local newspaper showing Carlos masquerading as a bullfighter during Carnival time, or a more unfortunate photograph from a magazine depicting him smoking or dancing in a cabaret, were promptly dispatched to my father as reinforced proof of my uncle's poor opinion of my brother as a student. He often added a sanctimonious footnote, saying, "You see, we parents work damn hard only for our children to throw our money away." My father wrote stern letters to my brother, threatening to cut his monthly allowance should he continue frequenting depraved places, as my father called them, and urging him to work harder at his studies.

My uncle's spying activities on my brother's life only served to strengthen my affection for Carlos. I always wrote to him promptly to warn him of my uncle's reports as soon as these reached home, when my father would predictably explode in a fit of rage and threaten to have my brother sent back home. On such occasions, money exchanged hands from my mother to me, and I slipped it in an envelope and sent it to my brother, to cushion out lean days before my father calmed down and relented once again, and sent him his usual allowance. Thus, a conspiratorial friendship blossomed between me and my brother.

My father was delighted to see his elder son home on his Silver Jubilee. As the two men embraced and patted each other on the back warmly, I detected once again a note of apprehension in my brother, and although I was eager to talk to him alone, the opportunity never arose. We were all swept away by the euphoria of the occasion.

Lunch was announced, and we all queued up for the large dining-room, where our eyes and appetite were regaled with a feast of the most imaginative dishes from the Cantonese and Portuguese cuisines. Piquant chicken *piri-piri* and *bacalhau de creme* vied with Cantonese roast duck and pork for the guests' favour. Chinamen whom I had known as teetotallers were washing their meal down with good doses of brandy and rice wine. Everybody ate like a glutton. And I observed that even the most beautiful people looked unattractive when they ate.

When coffee was served, my father gathered two of his best friends, Mr Lo and Mr Yan, around him and made what he believed to be a short and simple speech.

"Relatives, friends and colleagues," he began, "I would like to thank you all for coming today and sharing with me this very special occasion. When I look back over the past twenty-five years, I can sincerely say that I couldn't have made it without the support of my family and friends. I want to mention Mr Lo and Mr Yan especially, with whom I shared lodgings when I first arrived here in Beira, who were neighbours and friends when we lived in Maquinino, and whose business careers have followed similar paths to mine. We are known in social and business circles as the Maquinino Connection, and together we founded the Kuomintang and the Oriental Club here in Beira.

We have known and shared many moments of sorrow and happiness, and our children are the best of friends. I would like to take the opportunity of this very special occasion to announce how happy I, Mr Lo, and Mr Yan would be if any of our children should unite the three families through marriage and keep our good fortune in the family." At this public announcement, my father, Mr Lo and Mr Yan clapped and nodded, while their children blushed with embarrassment and the other guests chuckled, muttering between their teeth, "wishful thinking on the old man's part." "I propose a toast to you all," continued my father, "may peace, health, and prosperity be always with you. May I also count on your support and collaboration in the years to come." The guests rose to the toast, had a sip of coffee, clapped, and cheered.

In a corner of the hall, four men were standing in a cluster, three heads locked in petty conversation, whilst one kept a certain physical distance as if to dissociate himself from the conspiracy. And behind a façade of goodwill and applause, the cracks began to appear as my uncles Knight, Jovial, and Syrup schemed to discontinue their past collaboration with the patriarch in future business dealings.

"The bastard has grown fat on us. See what he already has, look at this house. And what have we got to show for our hard work?" complained my uncles Jovial and Syrup, first cousins of my father. "We must try and sell our salt fish and dry shrimps to someone else from now on, instead of allowing the patriarch to be our sole distributor. He has taken us too much for granted, and it's about time we took our produce elsewhere."

Uncle Knight rejoiced, saying, "And I will not buy my merchandise from him either."

Uncle Phoenix, my mother's brother, who had remained silent while the other three men conspired among themselves, butted in at this point and said, "Putting your pettiness aside, it is naïve of you to assume that you can get a better deal elsewhere. You can, of course, find another distributor for your fish and shrimps, but tell me, who will give you the credit facilities you now enjoy under your present arrangement with my brother-in-law? Who will supply you with the cash flow to cover your employees' wages, when the fishing seasons are bad, and your bank account is empty? Who would sell you on credit and in bulk basic commodities like maize flour, oil, soap, and sugar, which are compulsory supplements to your employees' wages? Think hard, and give me the name of a businessman who will offer you better terms than the ones you already enjoy. It is easy for you to talk big."

"Rubbish!" Uncle Knight exclaimed. "Of course Jovial and Syrup can and will find another distributor who will give them equally good terms, if not better than the ones they've been receiving from my brother. There are many Chinese businessmen who would be only too happy to trade with my cousins, and on terms favourable to them both. You'll see."

Years later, when my father discovered that his cousins had been selling him only half of their catch, he was incensed and took them to task, reminding them of their obligation and loyalty to the family as a whole. "If you wanted to sell your produce elsewhere, why didn't you sell the lot to someone else?" my father pressed Uncles Jovial and Syrup, and then added, "Because you wished to retain the credit facilities and the cash I allowed you to have, and which you couldn't get elsewhere, right?" My uncles were ashamed to have been thus exposed.

Uncles Jovial and Syrup joined my father in Africa after he had sent for his two brothers, Light and Knight, and Knight's wife, Peach Blossom, and son Ferryboat. Uncle Light died of tuberculosis in Beira three years after his arrival. Uncles Jovial and Syrup settled in Govuro, where they started a joint fishing business. Bachelor Jovial took up with two native women who bore him a handful of children, but when he felt the time had come for him to settle down and get married, he abandoned the two women as if they were cheap commodities to be discarded without ceremony, and sent for a wife from China. The matchmaker from his village of Hui Yin sent him a photograph of a good-looking woman sitting on a bench with her mother, and from the matchmaker's letter of recommendation, Jovial decided that the young woman in the photograph was good enough for him.

When she disembarked in Beira and walked down the gangplank to meet him, Uncle Jovial exclaimed, "Aiah! What have I done? What have I got myself into?"

And only then did he remember that he had forgotten to enquire from the matchmaker about his bride's height. And on occasions when our family gathered together for parties, and we children teased and bullied him into dancing with his wife, he would say, "Dancing with your Aunt Lotus Flower is like holding a chair," and then he would cackle.

Aunt Lotus Flower came to live with us when her first child was born. She confided to my mother that she could no longer bear to live in Govuro, where her husband's former women knocked regularly on her door demanding food. She chased them away, but they returned with the children and begged for food and clothes. They asked for *Muzungo* to take pity on his own sons. Uncle Jovial let them in, said Lotus Flower, gave them a meal, and then sent them away. Sometimes, my aunt complained, the women stayed on in the house long after the children had gone. As my aunt lived in our big house, she saw less and less of her husband, who travelled up to Beira only a few times a year to settle business matters with my father. And when her fourth child was five years old, Lotus Flower and her children moved into a flat of their own.

Uncle Syrup didn't stay in Govuro for too long. On one of his business trips to Beira, he met and fell in love with a black widow, who lived in the Esturro area in a small wooden house on stilts, surrounded by acres of banana trees. He moved in with her, and lived with her until his dying days. Rumour had it that she had bewitched him with love potions from her witchdoctor. Whenever I visited my uncle as a young adolescent, his voluminous companion always insisted with a hearty guffaw that I call her Aunt, and gave me a basketful of golden bananas, picked from her yard, to take home.

When Uncle Syrup was forty, our extended family urged him to get married to a woman of his own race, and pleaded with the black widow to set him free. She agreed to do so, provided my uncle married a girl of her choice. She selected for my uncle a young local Chinese woman whom she knew well and liked. But the young woman found my uncle too old for her taste and refused the marriage proposal. She married a photographer of her own age instead, only to regret her decision months later when she found herself regularly with a black eye. And Uncle Syrup went on living happily ever after in the magical house on stilts.

At sunset, the September sky was golden. From the veranda of our house, I watched the giant sun dive in majestic slow motion into the Indian Ocean. The guests were leaving, but close friends of the family and first cousins had been invited to stay for tea and a firework display.

The servants carried boxes of fireworks to the veranda, and the remaining guests crowded into the open air. I found a niche next to my father and brother Carlos, and held tightly to the handrail lest grown-ups jostled me out of my corner. My brothers lit the fireworks and flung them up into the air. They shot up a shower of colourful dragons and pagodas, silver-haired sages, and dancing maidens in flowing robes, fishing boys, and butterflies, and dipped and cast a smoky mist over the warm early evening. Amidst the ceaseless crackling of fireworks, my father suddenly remembered to ask my brother Carlos at what time he was flying back to Lourenço Marques the following afternoon.

"I am not going back," Carlos said. A heavy silence fell upon us. My father said nothing, buried his head in his chest and walked away from the veranda.

My mother threw Carlos a pained look and whispered, "Why did you do that? Why did you have to spoil his day like this? Why couldn't you have waited for the Christmas vacation to announce your decision?" Then she went indoors to look for my father.

I tugged at my brother's sleeve, and almost in tears, asked in a broken voice, "Why, Carlos? Why don't you want to go back to your studies?"

"Because I play the harmonica more than I study," he replied.

6

BEYOND THE SCARECROW

If I captured the hazy memories of my early childhood in hues of grey and red on the canvas of my mind, I painted my early girlhood in rich colours of green and yellow and blue, which blinded my senses in the limitless fields of my school holidays in Muda. There, I soaked my freedom-hungry spirit in a bright yellow sea of sunflowers that willingly surrendered its will to the magnet of the golden sun.

Around the time we moved into our new house, my Uncle Phoenix's fortunes were also in the ascendancy. And as a way of repaying my father for his three children's stay in our house during school terms, Uncle Phoenix made a point of inviting me to spend my school holidays at his house in Muda. He came to fetch us in his lorry, and we trucked up endless miles of savannah and bush until we reached the River Pungue. Here, we were chain-ferried across the river by a group of Shona ferrymen, who sang solemn, mournful songs about toil and death as they heaved and hoed. Once on dry land, we were greeted by further stretches of grassland, until half an hour's drive before we reached our destination, maize plantations began to appear on the horizon.

Uncle Phoenix ran a thriving general store, and was about to branch out into a small enterprise in sunflower oil extraction. At the time, his shop was the only one existing in Muda, a settlement of black and white smallholders, white plantation owners, Portuguese administrators and officials, and rural workers. Business for my uncle was brisk. From dawn to sundown, there was always noise and movement. Travellers journeying from the city of Beira to the interior of the country or to Southern Rhodesia, stopped in Muda to refill their tanks at my uncle's petrol station, have a drink in his bar, or just a snack to eat. Native women brought the fruits of their land and poultry to Uncle Phoenix's shop to barter for basic necessities, such as cotton cloths, salt, soap, paraffin, matches, and oil. Most of these women walked long distances to reach the shop and brought with them their lunch. And after they had bartered their own produce and eaten their lunch, they settled down for a siesta outside the shop, under the giant hibiscus tree.

My cousin Emília, Uncle Phoenix's daughter, and I skipped and hopped, and played with hula hoops in the front yard of my uncle's shop, in full view of the shoppers. Skinny legs hopping and shapeless hips swirling bright-coloured rings vigorously, we drew enthusiastic applause from the female audience who, contaminated by our gymnastic feats, ran back into the shop to purchase, on credit, skipping ropes and hula hoops on the understanding that these would be paid for with the produce of their land which they would bring next time. While the women were content with such simple items, the male wage-earners coveted with avid eyes the bicycles that Emília and I rode round and round the open space which surrounded my uncle's house, our wheels zigzagging under the tall coconut trees.

The night was never still. I was often woken from my sleep by the roaring of some wild animal in the near distance, or the chugging of the night freight train which came from Southern Rhodesia and stopped at the station, some two hundred yards away from the house, to load and unload some more cargo before resuming its journey to the port city of Beira.

After a siesta, Emília and I pedalled to my uncle's sunflower fields, which rolled away endlessly till the end of the earth. When we reached the edge of the field, we got off our bikes, dropped them unceremoniously on the grass, and ran wild in between the rows and rows of towering sunflowers. We played peekaboo, and popped our tanned faces out from behind the sturdy stalks of the sunflowers. And amid girlish giggles, we hopped and ran deeper and deeper into the fields. Aunt Flora had instructed us not to go too far, and certainly not beyond where the scarecrow had been planted, lest we should go astray and get lost in the field. But something mysterious and wicked beckoned us on and on. As I dashed forward to cross beyond where the scarecrow stood, I felt uneasily excited to be on the brink of a new discovery, but my cousin, only three weeks older than me, pulled me back and reminded me of her mother's warning. Aunt Flora said rumour had it that an evil spirit roamed around the fields in Muda, and as far as my uncle's sunflowers were concerned, this evil spirit had chosen to establish its territory in the fields beyond the scarecrow; but as long as we didn't go out of our way to seek it out, it would not harm us. "Don't trespass into the privacy of its chosen land, and you'll be safe," she stressed. Sulking, I stomped back to where Emília was standing. But once we got back to the demarcation line, I felt light again and, doing somersaults, cartwheels, and dizzying pirouettes, we made our way back to the safe grounds we had just covered.

Then, one glorious blue afternoon, when a giant round coin of pure gold was shining down precisely in a vertical line above my head, a dot suspended in infinity and hanging parallel to my throbbing heart, I wickedly whispered into my cousin's ear that today of all days, I was going to venture into the fields beyond the forbidden frontier. Without waiting for Emília's reaction, I darted away. "No, Estrela! Come back!" Her cries pierced the still heavy air which trapped my steps as I ran on and on among the sunflowers beyond the scarecrow. I parted endless green and yellow curtains as I moved further and further away from my cousin. My heart was thumping loud, but I didn't know exactly why. I didn't expect the sunflowers beyond the scarecrow to look different from those on the other side of the border, nor was I searching for some exciting hidden treasure. Perhaps I was afraid after all of actually confronting the demon, and therefore confirming the rumours about its existence on this side of the scarecrow. Engrossed in my own doubts, I pressed ahead, timidly pushing aside the thick foliage that dangled abundantly before my eyes.

Suddenly, a big throaty voice blared out, "Peekaboo!" I saw nothing but sunflowers, but sensed a presence around me. I stood still, my heart pounding in my ears. And from out of nowhere, a weird figure advanced towards me, some twelve feet away from where I stood, glued to the ground. His face was painted chalky white and his smudged popping eyes were defined by a circle of yellow dye. His gleaming torso was bedecked with colourful bead jewellery. He swayed his hips, swish-swishing his abundant straw skirt, and he punctuated the languid rhythm of his body movements with a shake of his coconut rattle. As he ambled and half-danced towards me, coming perilously nearer and nearer all the time, I noticed the skin on his large flat feet was dark, dusty, and wrinkled like that of an elephant. Suddenly, images of captured white men cooked alive in a giant cauldron by savage natives from some comic strip I had read, flashed through my mind, and I ran for my life. I saw the shadow of the weird figure follow me, and I screamed for help. I felt my lungs explode.

Emília was waiting for me at the very spot where I had left her. As we met, we joined hands together and ran. But no shadow pursued us any longer, and as we glanced back while running, we saw the stranger walk away and disappear among the sunflowers.

I was still trembling with fear when we arrived home. Aunt Flora placed a necklace with a jade charm around my neck to protect me from evil spirits, and tugging my ear, chanted repeatedly, "Fear no fear, fear no fear." She chided me gently for having disobeyed her instructions, and told us that the weird figure I had encountered beyond the scarecrow was a witchdoctor. "Is he, Aunt Flora, the evil spirit rumoured to inhabit the sunflowers beyond the scarecrow?" I asked. My aunt didn't reply to my question, but her silence neither denied nor confirmed it. After a brief pause, she observed, "Had you listened to my instructions and not probed further into the fields beyond the scarecrow, you would have been spared a nasty, frightening experience. Next time you are tempted to question what meets the ear, think again before you get yourself into trouble, do you hear? There are things in life that are best left alone." To comfort me, Aunt Flora cooked gazelle stew for supper; a favourite dish enriched with tomatoes and herbs freshly picked from her garden. She added a spoonful of grated fresh ginger root to tone down the gamey taste of the meat. And she mentioned that the meat had been delivered that same afternoon by her brother, a professional game hunter.

Uncle Phoenix was a warm and generous person. On his weekly trips to Beira to buy merchandise for his shop, he would bring us crates of home-grown golden mangoes, papayas, and guavas. And on Saturday evenings, he and Aunt Flora came down to Beira to see a Chinese film at the Chinese school, and Mother and I were always invited to go with them. Many of the films shown at the school were opera, and they were so popular with the audience that the spectators clapped and sang along with the stars in the film, aided by the words that were flashed onto the screen. Although at the time I couldn't read well in Chinese, I had a good ear and simply imitated the sounds that the grown-ups in the audience made. And so I began to develop a taste for Chinese opera, a form of mass entertainment, and subsequently became a lover of both Chinese and European opera.

At Christmas, Uncle Phoenix took Emília and me to the largest toyshop in town and bought us each a doll of our own choice as a Christmas present, regardless of the price. I tended to select one which had the opposite characteristics from my own, such as blonde hair and blue eyes, and made a point of taking one that cried whenever I tipped it over. And if the shop happened to stock only one doll of the kind that both Emília and I wanted, Uncle Phoenix coaxed his daughter to relent and let me have it, saying that it was a small sacrifice to make, considering that she was living in our house. The sacrifice, he explained to Emília, should be seen as a token of goodwill for all the years she had been raised in our house. Cousin Emília protested and grumbled, saying, "Why should I always be the one to make sacrifices? Why should Estrela always get her way?" But Uncle Phoenix only nudged her to silence, exclaiming, "Heh, heh, what is this? Where are your manners, Emília?"

Uncle Phoenix's attitude to life in general was easy going and carefree. But one thing distressed and worried him a great deal: his second son, Felipe. Together with his brother Miguel and sister Emília, Felipe also lived with us, but my parents were reluctant to have him. He played truant at school, was a difficult youth to cope with, and often stole money from my mother's housekeeping allowance. At first, my parents only reprimanded him and then excused him because he was a relative, and the amounts of money he pilfered were too small for my father to take any petty punitive action. But as he reached his late teens, he became involved with a group of local dropouts and delinquents, and collectively they organised and launched night-time robberies on various business premises. My parents were suspicious of Felipe's criminal activities, for he was always absent from the house whenever the robberies took place, and because he flaunted a considerable amount of cash, for which he couldn't account. But they remained silent, for they had no concrete evidence to prove their suspicions right, and above all, because of the shame a public admission of my cousin's criminal offences would bring to my family.

One Saturday evening, my parents went to the cinema at the Chinese School with Uncle Phoenix and Aunt Flora. Not enjoying the film, my father left halfway through it, and on the way home, decided to drop in at the office to pick up some accounts he had left unattended and which he wanted to look over the following morning. And there in the office he caught my cousin Felipe and his young friends red-handed as they were emptying the money from the safe. Felipe, living as he did in our house, had an inkling of where my father kept the keys to the office and safe, and as we were all out that evening, he and his friends had decided to steal the keys. Shocked that his own nephew should bite the very hand that fed him, my father saw no alternative but to report his disappointment to Uncle Phoenix, and ask him to remove his son permanently from our house. My father did not refer the matter to the police, and the whole incident was swept under the carpet. But tension and resentment began to build up between the two families, and although Cousin Emília went on living with us, her brothers returned home to Muda to live and work with their parents. And I no longer went back to Muda for my school holidays. I was growing up, too, and Muda became a memory that gradually faded from my mind as I rushed headlong towards my mid-teens.

Back in Muda, the two brothers bickered and quarrelled bitterly over who should have priority of choice in running the various businesses their father now held. They came to dislike and resent each other so much that eventually they confronted Uncle Phoenix, and openly demanded that he should choose an official heir to his business concerns. Having forced the issue, they wanted a prompt answer from their father, there and then. Hesitantly, Uncle Phoenix replied, "My children, the day will come when I shall divide my business enterprises and properties fairly between you two. But you are now both apprentices learning the ropes, and it is only fair that you should share the responsibilities of running my business equally. There is no one heir, official or unofficial, and you must learn to work together, instead of fighting each other. But since Miguel is the eldest of my children, it is only natural that I should expect him to shoulder a greater share of responsibility in the day-to-day running of my business affairs…" Before Uncle Phoenix could finish his speech, cousin Felipe, his angry face flushed red, stormed out of the house, and was never seen again.

The following morning, bits and pieces of his dismembered and decapitated body were found dispersed along the railway line by my uncle's house. He had thrown himself under the night freight train.

Aunt Flora never forgave my parents for having expelled her son from our house. She reasoned that if Felipe hadn't been sent away by my parents, he wouldn't have returned home to live in Muda in the first place, and therefore wouldn't have quarrelled with his brother and taken his own life. Aunt Flora never recovered from the violent manner in which her son died. And many years later, unable to bear the pain and grief of his death any longer, she took her own life by hanging herself in the bathroom. After two suicides, and with his sons' notorious wild tempers, Uncle Phoenix's family became known as unbalanced, suicide-prone, and insane. And innocent Cousin Emília became unmarriageable in the eyes of the families of possible suitors. As for Cousin Miguel, he too could not find a wife among the Chinese.

7

CRIES AND WHISPERS

I got back home from a clandestine rendezvous and tiptoed into the house, hoping not to run into anyone and be asked where I had been. When I reached the third flight of steps, I saw my sister-in-law Julie, Carlos's wife, who was watering her yucca plants on the landing. I felt trapped. But she merely said in a matter-of-fact way, "Ah, there you are! Your mother has been looking for you the whole morning. She wants to speak to you." And glancing at her wrist-watch, she added, "You know where to find her at this hour." She stared at the bright red hibiscus flower I had clipped in my hair and which I had forgotten to take off, and for a moment I thought I saw the corners of her lips curve downwards in a mocking, knowing smile. I darted up the stairs before she had time to utter another word, and proceeded directly to the roof-garden by way of the spiral indoor staircase.

I expected to find my mother in the roof-garden doing her usual chore, for although we now had several servants, my mother continued to perform some domestic tasks out of habit and, I think, therapeutic necessity.

She was sitting on the stone steps with a rush colander on her lap. I stood still on the landing, watching her, afraid of breaking the magic of that tranquil moment captured in the serenity of her face and gestures. She tossed the grains of rice into the air, and as they fell in the colander, she swept them loose with her bare hand right across the width of the receptacle. The rice dust filtered through the fine mesh, and she picked out coarse husks, which she discarded as unfit for consumption. Then she repeated the process all over again, tossing the grains in the sun. The calm concentration she exercised on such a simple activity kept in check the turbulent thoughts she never let out, but which were always close to the surface. For in her pain, my mother was self-contained.

"I must tell your brother that this consignment of rice is of very poor quality," she remarked, without turning her head in my direction.

I sat next to her quietly. The fragrance of the flowers filled the golden air, and I lifted my face towards the clear blue sky, drinking in the warm sunbeams which seeped through the bougainvillea vault above my head.

"You've just come back from the beach," she said, without looking at me or pausing from what she was doing. I was about to answer "no", but held my tongue in time as I glanced down at my sand-sprinkled toes showing through my open sandals.

"You know how much you upset your father, sneaking off to the beach so often."

"Oh, Mother, just because two of my siblings drowned at the beach many years ago, it doesn't follow that a similar fate will strike me. Besides, I go to Macuti Beach, and never to the one that has lots of whirlpools, where brother and sister died."

"You know *that* is not what I mean."

"What then?"

"You know exactly what I mean. Chico. You went to meet him at the beach, didn't you?"

I made no reply.

"Estrela, we need to talk about your relationship with Chico. Your father has asked me to speak to you. You know that neither your father nor I have anything against Chico as a person. In fact, I like him. He is hard-working, well-mannered, and clean-cut. But you know the position. His parents are divorced, and his mother is having an affair not only with a married man, but a mulatto on top of that. Now, this is just not acceptable among good, respectable families. Your father wants you, asks you, to end your relationship with Chico. By all means remain friends when you run into each other, but don't bring him home. You know how people gossip in a small city like this. You'll just win yourself a bad reputation and spoil your chances of making a good marriage one day if you go on seeing him. And you know how many good families have already asked your father for your hand in marriage. Your father will never allow you to marry Chico, because such a marriage would only bring shame and dishonour to your family. Your father has, in fact, ordered me to order you never to see Chico again. And you know what that means. If you disobey me, he'll only get it out on me. If you pity me, then you'll do as he tells you, Estrela."

"Yes, Father would exploit my love for you to blackmail me, wouldn't he?" I said serenely... "You know that I will never allow him to hurt you if I can help it. And he knows that."

I walked to the parapet and peered down to where our servants' quarters were. Joaquim, our *mainato*, was crouched over a drain in the stone yard, and was brushing his teeth vigorously with a hibiscus twig. He stopped brushing, held the brown stick in the air, rinsed his mouth with water from a tin mug, and spat out a mouthful of clear yellowish juice. He then stuck out his bright pink tongue and scraped it with a broader twig.

Not far from Joaquim sat my four-year old nephew, Bernardo, on a low wooden stool. He was watching his little black boy cooking and stirring a lunch of maize flour in a tin pot over an open fire. From time to time, he got up, walked up to the fire, and stuck his index finger in the cooking pot to test the consistency of the flour. And sucking his smeared finger, he chuckled with the black boy and then sat back on his stool. My photographic mind wandered from the tall wall, which enclosed the back of our house and servants' compound, to the horizon, where the Indian Ocean and infinity blended as one. In quiet exasperation, I turned round to face my mother and sighed, "Oh, the heat and small-town people! And nothing else. How I'd like to get out of here!"

"Come now, my daughter, you are exaggerating. What about the beach, the bougainvillea, and the sunflowers you love so dearly? What about the winter seasons that chase the heat away? And what about your brothers and sisters and friends who love you, and whose affection counterbalances the narrow mentality of the people here? You know, Estrela, life has its own rhythm. The anger and impatience one feels in youth mellow with age, and one acquires the serenity to cope with the world as it is. Not with the world as one thinks it should be. There is a relative sequence to one's time – a time to love, a time to die, and a time to venerate. Everything will fall into place, you'll see."

I plucked a cluster of jasmine flowers, inhaled their sweet perfume deeply, and ambled back to where my mother remained seated.

"I'm going abroad one day. Soon."

"You've been saying that ever since you were fifteen, and you are still here, Estrela. Doesn't that say something?"

"You needn't worry about me and Chico. It is unlikely we'll ever see each other again. This guerrilla war is engulfing us all, and goodness knows what will become of us. I am so glad Luís will be home from military service next week. Four years is a long time. I doubt he'll ever want to get back to his studies.

Chico is returning to Salisbury next week, and I don't think he'll ever come back to Beira."

"Oh, really? Why?"

"His mother wants him to stay put in Rhodesia because of military service. She fears that if he comes back home for holidays, the authorities here might stop him from returning to Salisbury, and recruit him for national service instead. Quite a few students have been refused permission to extend their exemption from military service. To be safe, Chico will remain in Salisbury until he has completed his medical studies. Besides, it is not only you and Father who want our relationship terminated. Chico's mother has also asked him to stop seeing me. She doesn't like me. If only your generation were subtle enough, you'd realise that our relationship would have petered out as a matter of course. There was no need for Father to warn me – that would only have enticed the rebel in me to challenge his authoritarian rule and continue with the relationship for the sake of proving my own independence."

"Why doesn't Chico's mother like you?" my mother asked, offended.

"Come, come, Mother! Don't tell me your pride is wounded!" I teased her. "Oh, she doesn't like me, that's all. You know how proud and possessive she is over her precious doctor son. She'll get jealous over any girl who happens to hold Chico's affection. In her jealousy, she'll find any pretext to dislike the poor girl. She says I'm not the right girl for her son, because she is obsessed with physiognomy, like most of the China women here, and interprets certain of my physical characteristics as being ominous. My high forehead, she says, is a sign that I'm a domineering person, and wouldn't therefore make an obedient and dutiful daughter-in-law. My large wide mouth means I'll eat up my husband's fortune, and my small, narrow hips mean I cannot bear any children. You know, old wives' tales."

"She talks nonsense," my mother responded, outraged. "Every prospective mother-in-law who has asked for your hand in marriage has remarked how well balanced and regular your facial features are. You have such a peaceful countenance, and the Chinese like this. To look at peace with oneself is a commendable feature when choosing a bride, and augurs well for marriage. But your greatest asset, Estrela, lies in your legs, because they are slim and aristocratic."

"Oh, Mother," I laughed. "You peasants are snobs, aren't you? Fancy talking about aristocratic legs."

"Don't joke about it, my daughter, and don't underestimate what I've just said."

"In my generation, we don't pay any attention to old wives' tales and superstitions. And when we marry, we marry for love, warts and all. I'm not so naïve as to believe that love solves all problems, and I'm aware there are countless other reasons why a marriage should go wrong. But anyway, why are we talking of marriage now? I have no intention of getting married for many years to come. And when I do get married, I don't want to marry a family and end up like my sisters. I'd rather die an old maid than marry a family."

"But that's the point, Estrela. Parents are always concerned about the family their children marry into. It is why we were concerned about your relationship with Chico. If you select a good, generous family, there is no reason why you shouldn't live happily and harmoniously with your new family."

"That doesn't make sense, Mother. How can one ever tell whether the family one has selected is a generous one? Only time can prove or disprove it, in which case it would be futile, since one would have been married into the family anyway. I prefer a system whereby I marry a man for himself and live with him alone, and not for and with his entire family, like ours is."

I heaved a sigh of grief as I thought of my sisters Sofia and Clara. Sofia married for love, and Clara for the sake of marrying, and both won themselves a family of bullies and thugs.

Sofia married into a family poorer than her own, and with my father's reluctant blessing. As an act of punishment and revenge against Sofia's higher social position, her widowed mother-in-law and unmarried sisters-in-law, who still lived in the same house, bullied her and made her scale fish in the presence of her new relatives, as a demonstration that a rich girl (as they now called her with contempt) could and did work with her hands. Not satisfied with this public humiliation, Sofia's in-laws made her cook every day, twice a day, for the whole household, when she returned home from her full-time job as a secretary. Independent Sofia would not acquiesce, and rebelled against her family's tyranny. She pleaded with her husband to leave his mother's house and set up a home of their own, but he said, "Why are you trying to drive a wedge between my family and me?" After Sofia had threatened to leave with or without him, he agreed reluctantly to move into a flat of their own, but as a show of loyalty to his family, he did not speak to his own wife for one whole year. And in the history of the local Chinese community, Sofia became known as a bossy wife.

Clara was in her mid-twenties when a Chinese trader in Southern Rhodesia asked for her hand in marriage through a go-between. As my parents and relatives feared that at her age, she might end up on the shelf if she refused this opportunity to get married, they pressurised her into accepting the proposal, even though they were aware she was marrying into a family ruled by a wanton tyrant who enjoyed humiliating people for the sake of it.

Clara's mother-in-law had been only sixteen years old and bearing a child when her husband died. The young widow had struggled hard to earn a living and bring up her son alone, and in the long process had become embittered and vengeful. When her son got married, she had already built herself a materially comfortable life, but had become so brutalised by what she perceived as the merciless hands of destiny that she felt the sadistic need to avenge her former harsh life by abusing her newly-married daughter-in-law. Clara became a full-time housewife and did her duties according to her mother-in-law's precise instructions. But for every dish she cooked which was not to her mother-in-law's personal satisfaction, Clara was made to apologise and kneel down on the kitchen floor for a long period of time. Once, she had to remain on her knees from eight in the morning to five in the afternoon without food or water, and as she was pregnant, she fainted with exhaustion. The following day, Clara escaped from home and caught a train back to Beira, to find sanctuary at her former home. And although my parents believed and accepted Clara's stories about her mother-in-law's maltreatment of her, they felt it was their duty to send her back to her husband once the baby was born. "You are a married woman now, daughter, and you belong to your husband's family now," my parents explained to Clara, "and since they want you and your baby back with them, it is our duty not to interfere with their wishes, in the same way that we wouldn't like our daughter-in-law's parents interfering with ours. You understand our Chinese ways, don't you?" my parents coaxed her further. In the end, Clara's husband travelled down to Beira to claim his wife and child, and they returned with him to Salisbury. After Clara's second child was born, her husband quarrelled with his mother over an insignificant matter, such as a new cradle for the newly-born. And bottled-up feelings of anger, which he had nurtured and stored away against his own mother over the years, finally burst into the open. Mother and son exchanged bitter, intractable words, and finally the mother walked out to live with friends. Gossip had it that Clara quarrelled with her mother-in-law and expelled her from her own house. And my parents gained the unenviable reputation of having produced two very bossy wives.

"Now, Estrela, I admit that neither of your sisters married into an ideal family, but you, you couldn't possibly be unhappy with either Sérgio's or César's families. They are our closest friends and allies, and they have loved you since you were a child. You know that Mr Lo and Mr Yan have asked your father, on their sons' behalf, for permission to marry you. Your father approves both of them. The choice is yours."

"Mother, really! Sérgio and César and I understand why you old dears want to see our families united through a marriage bond, but we, your children, have our own plans. I like Sérgio and César very much, because we are childhood friends. We grew up together and played together, and are like brothers and sister, but when it comes to marriage, I don't want a brother, nor they a sister. Sérgio is happy living in New York and, from what he tells me in his letters, is dating a Chinese American psychology student whom he hopes to marry when he has completed his PhD. He jokes in his letters that the girl's parents are not too keen on what they call his 'African yokel' background, but given time, I'm sure the snobs will relinquish their prejudice. As for César, he is happy in Hong Kong, and dating a Taiwanese student. And I want to go to Europe."

"I see you children certainly have your own plans. Mr Lo and Mr Yan and your father will be very disappointed."

"I bet they will. Going back to what you were saying earlier on, about the desirability of marrying into a generous family as a solution to harmonious living, I think a married couple need to live on their own, independently of their in-laws, so as to have space and time to themselves, to grow. I agree we must help look after our in-laws, especially in their old age, but I don't approve the kind of set-up where various families live as one household under the same roof. Like ours, for instance. I am sure you and Father perceive yourselves as being kind and generous to Julie, and soon to Luís's wife. But equally, your daughter-in-law must have her own grievances for having to live under the same roof as me and my cousins, who will be remaining here for as long as we are unmarried."

"How typical of you to only mention the negative side of our traditions, Estrela. And what about the positive side? You know, there are many advantages to living in an extended family like ours. Instead of what you refer to as potential oppression and tyranny from the ruling parents-in-law, a married couple could enjoy the wisdom and protection of their elders. And think of the benefits children get from living with their grandparents. Adults may not get on together, but a child is always loved by the grandparents, and vice-versa. And a young mother can learn so much from her mother-in-law.

"Traditions, Estrela, have a logic of their own, and life its own unhurried seasons. We are a daughter, a daughter-in-law, a mother, a mother-in-law, and a grandmother at different stages of our pilgrimage on earth. And during this journey, we have a scale of duties to perform. We women attain a position of relative power and privilege when we become head of the female population in a household. And we also learn that together with this power goes the exercise of generosity, wisdom, and clemency. It is these attributes which make a good traditional mother-in-law and a harmonious family. I'm talking about the virtues of our Chinese ways."

"I know, Mother. But I wouldn't want to measure my life in terms of duties. I'm too individualistic to survive in a set-up full of rituals like that. I want to be myself, to create, to express myself, and be self-fulfilled. I would need personal freedom to be able to create situations which are beautiful to me. In your traditional model of conformity, the seeds of abuse, exploitation, cruelty, repression, and revenge are always there. And the dark side of the human heart can easily win in the ritual dance of duties."

A long pause ensued between us before I brought myself to speak again. My mother was helping herself to sweets from a tin sitting beside her.

"Mother," I reproached her, "you shouldn't be eating so many sweets. You are supposed to be on a diet, and your doctor has specifically instructed you not to eat sweets because of your diabetes. And high blood pressure." I closed the tin and was about to remove it from the stone steps where my mother was sitting, when she abruptly snatched it from me, clutched it on her lap, and scolded me. "Don't you tell me what I ought to eat or not. And to hell with the doctor's prescriptions. When I was young, I was healthy but poor. We hardly had anything to eat, and our diet was mainly vegetables. Now that I am materially comfortable and have plenty to eat, I have diabetes and must go on a diet. What an absurd twist of fate. Well, if I am to die, and I shall have to die one day, I might as well die well fed rather than hungry. I don't care what the doctor, my husband, and you children say, but I am going to eat what I please and die because of it."

I was moved by my mother's outburst, and understood her reasoning. I put my arm around her, and said with affection, "Yes, I agree, Mother. But you take care, won't you?"

"Contrary to what you may expect, Estrela," my mother continued, "I never felt ill-treated as much by my widowed mother-in-law. Of course, I had to work very hard. I used to get up early in the mornings to fetch water from a well, milk the goat, and prepare breakfast for the whole family. I served breakfast to the men first, who ate early and then set off to work in the field. I then served my mother-in-law, who got up a little later, and only after she had taken her breakfast would I sit down for mine. I was always the last to have my meals, so you can say I always had what was left over. After breakfast, I fed the poultry and pigs which we raised to sell in the market in town, washed clothes, swept and cleaned the house, and then prepared meals once more – a light lunch, and something more substantial for the evening meal. I did a lot of sewing and made most of the clothes for the family. The most painful chore of the day was to fetch warm water for the men to wash their feet with when they returned home from the field, and to wait on them in case the water temperature wasn't to their satisfaction, in which case I had to boil more water. I felt entirely at their mercy. Your Uncle Knight was the unkindest of my brothers-in-law. He frequently boxed my ears, complaining that the water was too cold, and from time to time, even bullied me into washing his feet. Then they all laughed at me in a chorus. That was the greatest humiliation I experienced in my married life in China. If and when I complained to my mother-in-law or to your father, your uncles turned even nastier and made life even more difficult for me. So in the first year of my marriage, I bore the insults in silence, and just got on with my daily chores. When I got heavily pregnant, my mother-in-law decided that the time had come for the men to fetch their own water. By the time my son was born, the men were so busy fetching their own water that they no longer remembered to pass the chore back to me."

I had a gut feeling that today, for the first time, my mother wished to open her heart and reveal herself to me. So although I wanted to comment on her condition as an oppressed woman in China, I did not interrupt her.

"After my family had accepted your father's marriage proposal, I went to the village temple to have my fortune read. The spiritual messenger sketched for me, with an ink brush, two roses on two separate branches full of thorns. The two branches were poised parallel to each other. She then interpreted the meaning of her sketch, saying that the thorns meant that my husband-to-be and I would lead a life riven with hardship and difficulties, and that the two roses on separate branches meant that our emotional lives would always run parallel to each other, like the two rose branches, but would never touch each other at any one point in space and time. To this very day, what she predicted has proved right."

My mother spoke in whispers, and her voice sounded broken by a quiet pain and regret. I did not dare to speak lest, in my empathy, I should utter platitudes. I listened with a mixture of pain and embarrassment.

"After we got married," my mother continued, "your father and I paid a visit together to the soothsayer in the temple. He predicted we would have many children, and the gods would allow us to have as many girls as we wished, but only two boys would remain ours in the end. So every time a boy was born to us, we wondered in fear about the fate of our newly-born. The gods played such havoc with our lives. Shortly after my twin girls were born, your father sailed for Africa to look for work. I brought up the children almost single-handed. My mother-in-law's help and support at this crucial period of our lives was invaluable. The need for survival united us, and we didn't have to keep remembering our respective ranks. We were just two mortals struggling to stay alive, body and soul. Your father wrote regularly, but his letters spoke of similar hardships and bouts of loneliness in the dark new land. He couldn't find a regular job and had to live on seasonal earnings whenever he could.

"When I arrived in Africa, Beira was a tiny egg of a town, dusty and underdeveloped. Although life was very harsh, I had a sense of purpose and direction in my life. I had a shop of my own to run, a family to look after, and even a social life of my own, without being trampled on or hounded by the demands of in-laws.

"I remember the excitement I felt on my first outing to the circus with the wives of the Chinese hopefuls who settled in this town around the same time as your father. There existed between us women a strong bond of solidarity and mutual help. We needed it to survive in our new and strange environment. I remember how we giggled silly as we donned European clothes for the outing, and wore white nylon stockings and high heels. And at the interval, we bought European sweets and chocolates to eat, and roamed around the grounds where the circus troupe had pitched its temporary home, wondered at the next destination of the colourful, neatly parked caravans, and marvelled at the caged lions from a safe distance, while the child audience pulled funny faces at the chimpanzees."

"Yes," I ventured to say, "I often picture your journey to Africa, from your little rural China, as a move into Babylon."

My mother laughed, without disagreeing with my observation.

"Of the friends I made at the time," she went on to say, "Pearl became the closest. And although she already had six children of her own by the time you were born, she loved you very much and asked to be your godmother. Estrela, there is something your father and I have never told you, but I think the time has now come for you to know it. You are old enough to understand. It was Pearl who literally brought you up during the first nine months of your existence. When you were born, you were my thirteenth child. I seemed to be always getting pregnant, and my children dying around me. Your brother, who had been born exactly a year before you and on exactly the same date, had just died. His death was declared accidental by the authorities, but I never quite forgave myself for it. You see, I was bathing him one evening and fainted with exhaustion, and he slipped and drowned immediately. I was barely recovering from the shock when I found myself pregnant again. I was physically and emotionally worn out, and resented and cursed your birth. I didn't even want to look at you or hold you, and was unmoved by your crying and helplessness. Pearl came to the house to bottle feed you, clean you, and tuck you into the cradle. Your brother Luís, who was five years old at the time, adored you, and in his possessive child love used to lock you and himself in the bedroom whenever Pearl called at the shop to see you.

'Please, let me in to feed your baby sister, Luís. It is far past her feeding time, and she must be very hungry,' Pearl pleaded.

But Luís would only reply, "Go away, she's mine and you can't take her away from me," clutching you so tightly in his arms that he almost asphyxiated you. You cried from discomfort, and Luís cried because he couldn't understand why you were crying. Pearl pleaded and bargained with Luís until he relented and unlocked the bedroom door. There were always noisy scenes and crying from your brother, but I remained lethargic and didn't want to have anything to do with you.

"'Why is your heart so dark?' Pearl chided me one day. 'Haven't you mourned enough for the loss of your baby son, and above all your own guilt? If you really hate the sight of your baby daughter so much, then let me adopt her. I will love her as my own.'

"Slowly but surely, I began to awaken from my numbness. I felt ashamed and remorseful for the way I had neglected you. I set out to put things right and make it up to you. But I was so guilt-ridden that I was never sure whether I was giving you enough love. I wanted to love you more and more, and in the clumsy process of doing so, I spoilt you instead. You know how I have always let you have your own way and excused you for your naughtiness, disobedience, and bad behaviour."

"You need never apologise to me, Mother. I understand. Anyone would," I said, "and if you have over-loved me and spoilt me because of those guilty feelings alone, your love has always been welcome and appreciated."

"It is just as well that the baby who died before you were born was a boy and not a girl. Had it been a girl, she would have begrudged your birth as a compensation for her death, and would have avenged your birth by pursuing and haunting you with misfortunes through the rest of your life. Whereas a baby of the opposite sex welcomed your birth as a continuation of his own life, and would therefore bless your life with good fortune as a way of fulfilling his own, had he lived. Ah, Estrela, you are smiling at me in disbelief. Call it peasant superstition or what you like, but in my China, this is what we believed." After a short pause, my mother said, smiling: "It is my hope to see you well married before the gods send for me. I want you to know that I've made some provision for you in case I die before you get married. I wouldn't want to see you financially dependent on your brothers or, more likely, on your sisters-in-law. Of course, you'll always have your brothers' love, but they have their own families to think about and won't always have time to remember you as a kid sister. I'm sure your father will see to your welfare, but just in case…"

"But, Mother, you forget that I have a job of my own, and am quite capable of looking after myself."

"Yes, but you'll need a red envelope to pad out your wardrobe. I gave one to Sofia and Clara when they got married, and I don't see why you should be an exception. Of course, if you choose not to get married, the red envelope will help you to maintain your independence. In spite of what I said about the good points of our Chinese ways, I agree with you on your insistence on individual independence. You see, I'm not *that* old-fashioned, or a rigid traditionalist. I want you to have the opportunities and education I never had. As Sofia is the eldest of my children, I have already told her where to find the lacquer box when the time comes. It is my inheritance to you. Under no circumstances can the lacquer box be opened before my death. These are verbal instructions I gave your father and Sofia. You must remind them, when the occasion arises. It is why I am telling you now."

"You will live for a long time yet, Mother. I might even surprise you with more grandchildren to add to your present collection."

"That will be the day, knowing you the way I do," she said. "You know, Estrela, your father has been a good husband, in spite of everything." I nodded, a little awkward to hear confirmed what I suspected she meant by "in spite of everything".

Often, in the misty-coloured memories of my childhood, I saw a dark-haired woman with a pale complexion, wearing a cream-coloured crêpe-de-chine dress, silk stockings, and white heeled shoes. She was no longer young, but well preserved. She held a white parasol in her gloved right hand, and with her left hand, she flirted, and coaxed my clumsy father along twisting paths in her orange grove, whispering softly about this tree or that. And I innocently followed them, her expensive perfume reeking from every pore of her body. I heard it whispered that this mysterious woman was a man-eater and maybe a widow, who clawed every *escudo* she could from any man in town, rich or poor, as long as he was still potent. It was why she could afford to live in luxurious surroundings, they said.

Once, when I went into my father's room and accidentally opened an old biscuit tin, hidden under a pile of letters tied by a string, I came across a black and white photograph showing a row of Chinamen sitting on chairs, another of men standing behind it, and yet another of men crouching in front of it. In a sea of male faces, only one female stood out, sitting in the middle row, flanked on her left by a man I did not know, and on her right by my father. And I recognised her as the woman in the orange grove. Upon this discovery, and afraid of being caught fiddling with my father's belongings, I hurried out of the room, and with my cheeks flushing, I stumbled on his toes as I left. My father was about to enter his room, and seeing me so embarrassed, gave me a puzzled look, but did not detain me to ask what I had been up to. In my haste, I left the photograph on top of the pile of letters instead of underneath it. The following day, my father gave me a stern, reproachful look, but never commented on the incident.

"Your father is not only a self-made man, but a self-taught one, too," my mother said, "and for an educated woman with a university degree and a teaching post, that can be an aphrodisiac."

"Why do you torture yourself like this, Mother? And me too? Don't you know that it pains me to hear you explain Father's current involvement with Miss Chiu? The question of aphrodisiacs doesn't come into this at all, Mother. Miss Chiu is already thirty-four years old, and desperate to grab a man. Father happened to be there. Had it been someone else, she would have gone after him, too. You shouldn't underestimate yourself, and you certainly needn't fear Miss Chiu. The Miss

Chiu you see is only her public persona. She may be educated, but she isn't as invulnerable, secure, and confident as she appears to be. I discovered she only came to Africa because her own widowed father had remarried, and to someone much younger than herself. According to Miss Chiu, her stepmother is a spoilt young woman who only worries about clothes and her manicured nails. Miss Chiu felt that her father no longer had time for her, and as she was getting on, she decided to try her luck abroad. Come to think of it, she may give herself airs, but she just has a job, like many of us. Nothing outstanding, really! You ought to remember this whenever you lose your self-confidence and start comparing yourself with her. Miss Chiu makes a lot of noise about her so-called scholarly abilities, doesn't she?

"You never went to university, and you don't hold a degree because you never had the opportunity to do so. But you are a self-made woman, Mother, and without you behind him, Father would never have got where he is now. And he knows it. Isn't this just as important as a piece of paper that states one has passed certain exams with a certain grade? You are a very modest person, but I don't think you should underestimate your own achievements."

Words stumbling over one another, I hastened to add clumsily, "When Miss Chiu arrived here in Beira, Father decided that I should take private classes in Chinese with her, because I went to a Portuguese school and couldn't write in Chinese. Miss Chiu and I got on well because she was a kind teacher to me. But she is really not a friend of mine. She lends me Chinese magazines because she thinks I should read as much Chinese as possible. That's why she seeks me out so often."

Tears welled up in my mother's eyes, rolled down her cheeks, and fell in pools on her spotted lap.

Miss Chiu's father was a functionary at the Ministry of Education in Taiwan, and she had come to Beira to teach Mandarin at the local Chinese primary school. She lived in the school's premises, and as my father was at the time chairman of the Chinese Association, which was responsible for the administration of the school, Miss Chiu and my father inevitably had a lot of contact with each other. As she knew no-one when she first arrived, my parents welcomed her into our home, and soon Miss Chiu became a regular visitor to the house. My sister-in-law Julie, who was a university graduate from South Africa, found she had many interests in common with Miss Chiu, and as they were both outsiders in their new homeland, they gradually developed a strong sense of solidarity between them and became good companions. And so Miss Chiu had an additional reason for being a frequent visitor to our house.

Miss Chiu was a good conversationalist, and for a businessman like my father with no formal education in Chinese literature, her knowledge, no matter how ossified, and her verbose tongue, fascinated him. She lent him books from her collection, and he lent her Chinese newspapers from Hong Kong, to which he subscribed. Whenever he wanted to read a good book, he consulted her, and she obligingly recommended a list.

They had discussions on the merits and weaknesses of the books they both read, often over lunch and supper in our house. My mother kept her cool, never betraying the unrest that now permeated her mind and threatened her existence. She received Miss Chiu's visits with politeness, and Miss Chiu reciprocated with rehearsed friendliness. But at our dining-table, with every shot she delivered from her pretentious analysis of a favourite poem, Miss Chiu aimed at dragging my father away from his wife and killing off, step by step, my mother's self-esteem and confidence. Anticipating victory, her predatory nostrils flared triumphantly. And so, from my early teens, I began to learn that women are the worst enemies to their own sex and to themselves.

My mother's friends called at the house, whispering stories about my father's weekly disappearances into Miss Chiu's flat at the back of the Chinese School. My mother bore her pain well and never raised the subject with her husband or children. More and more frequently, my father said that he had to deliver some newspapers for Miss Chiu, but that he would be back in time for supper. But supper came and went, and no sign of Father. "The food is getting cold and the grandchildren too hungry to wait," my mother said. And without further comment or fuss over my father's absence, my mother led the procession to the dining-room. By the time my father returned home, we had all retreated to the sitting-room for coffee. When my father appeared sheepishly in the sitting-room and mumbled some excuse or other for being late, my mother remained inscrutable. Gradually, I noticed that my mother ceased to care whether her husband supped at home or not.

My mother's initiative to thaw out her frozen heart on that Easter morning heralded, I believed then, an impending reconciliation with my father. But I was wrong. Apart from exchanging words with each other when absolutely necessary, a veil of silence fell between them. They continued going out together for social functions, but in the company of friends and visitors, they only spoke to each other indirectly. And at siesta time, my mother came to my bedroom for a rest, pitching a folding bed in the corner of the room by my wardrobe.

My mother's death four months later furnished me with some painful clues as to why she had finally decided to open her heart to me. She had felt her death coming, or perhaps she had deliberately courted it by plunging herself into an orgy of food consumption, selecting particularly the kind of rich, calorie-laden food her doctor had forbidden. No amount of pleading from her concerned children would dissuade her from eating what she so capriciously chose to eat.

Inevitably, the day came when it became too late to arrest the amount of sugar in her blood. And when my mother was hospitalised, my father chose to stay by her side, day and night, shoulders drooped by the heavy weight of guilt and neglect. My aunts Lotus Flower and Flora called at the private clinic to check on my mother's rapid deterioration, and frisked her body, especially her toes, for any sign of the final hour. Outraged by their physical violation and disrespect for the dying, my elder brother, fearing a similar mishandling of my mother's body by other equally insensitive relatives, decided to block all of them from entering my mother's room.

Late one afternoon, when my brothers and sisters and I gathered around my mother's bed and asked her how she was feeling, she pointed past us and said, "Look, there they are! My other children and relatives... they are all beckoning and calling me..." And pointing at the door of her room, she babbled on, "Nephew Felipe has just come in. He is sticking his tongue out at me." My brothers and sisters and I exchanged glances, and in the clinical quiet of the room, we knew the final hour was fast approaching. Suddenly, my father burst out crying, thrusting himself upon my mother. Torrents of tears tumbled down like white jade drops on my mother's bed sheet. It was chilly on that July evening.

After the funeral, close relatives congregated in our house for tea. Uncle Phoenix broke down in tears and vowed aloud, "I swear I will never set foot in this house again, now that my sister is dead!" We all knew what was on his mind. For it was the talk of the Chinese community that an eligible widower like my father would remarry in due course. And everyone was betting on Miss Chiu as the future bride. My father rebuked my uncle, reminding him that he would always remain a member of our large family, in spite of my mother's death. And there and then, to our surprise and disbelief, my father announced that he would never remarry.

I often asked myself why he had taken that decision, but he certainly kept true to his word. An unfaithful husband during my mother's lifetime, my father became faithful to her memory. With her death, my mother bound him forever to her.

Miss Chiu went on borrowing newspapers from my family whenever she came to visit us, but my father no longer went over to her flat to deliver them, nor did he consult her about books. One evening after supper, as Miss Chiu was leaving our house, she paused at the threshold and confided to me, "You know, Estrela, it has always been a platonic relationship between your father and me. You must believe me—" I interrupted her and said, "You really needn't explain and apologise. It isn't relevant or important now. It is ironic, isn't it, that in dying, my mother has unwittingly chained my father to her memory. You must feel cheated. She couldn't have inflicted a worse punishment on you, but you deserve it for the predatory way you treated her. I really am sorry for you." I felt precociously old as I uttered these words.

Two years later, Miss Chiu, finding no other outlet, settled for a Portuguese policeman who only had primary education.

After my mother's death, her seat at the dining-table, a plate and cutlery, were always kept intact for her, as if she might drop in for meals with us on any day. Many a time we felt a presence in our dining-room, and, on these occasions, my little nephew Bernardo would chuckle towards a specific direction, as if someone were standing there in the room and pulling funny faces at him, or tickling him under the arm. As for my father, he spent his free time solely for his grandchildren as a gesture of atonement for his past sins.

A week after the funeral, I inherited my mother's lacquer box, just as she had wished. Inside it, there lay curled up a silk caterpillar. I lifted the long, knotted green silk scarf out of the box and untied the knots. Inside each knot that my mother had tied, I found bank notes, which she had so patiently saved up over the years. South African gold rands lined the bottom of the box and its side pockets. When my father saw the contents the lacquer box, he got angry and said, "So this is how she stashed away the money she stole from me."

"No, Father, she did not steal your money, she earned it," Sofia chided my father, and she added, "Besides, much of the money was given to her over the years by her own brother as a gift. Mother has passed it down to Estrela as a safeguard to protect her independence. She was concerned that when you remarried, Estrela, being still single, might be regarded as a burden living under your and her brothers' roof."

"Why did she have to think the worst of me? Wouldn't I have made provisions for my own daughter? Why did your mother have so little faith in me?"

"It was just a precaution she took," my sister Sofia reassured my father. "As a businessman yourself, you must agree that she was right not to take chances."

When my Aunt Flora heard that her husband had given money to his sister consistently over the years, she wailed and cursed him for giving away what they had jointly earned as a result of so much sweat and hard work. So, amid much ill-feeling and angry words, I became an heir to a padded lacquer box.

8

SWEET AND SOUR

I promised my mother I would meet Chico only once more to bid him a final farewell. I enlisted my friend Isabel's help, and we came up with a plan that she should invite me to a matinée at the São Jorge cinema as a cover for my secret rendezvous with Chico. She would pick me up at my house and we would drop in at the Café Empório for tea before going to the cinema, she would tell my father. In this way, we found an additional pretext to prolong my meeting with Chico. As Isabel was my godmother's youngest daughter and a friend of the family, our outing to see a film on a weekday did not arouse my father's suspicions, nor did he query further the motive behind Isabel's invitation.

We normally went to the matinées on Sunday afternoons only, after a morning of weeding in the roof-garden or swimming at the beach, and a traditional Chinese lunch at home. My father insisted on the ritual of a Chinese lunch, explaining that at least once a week we, his children and grandchildren, ought to remind ourselves of our origins, our roots. For Sunday lunch, only genuine Chinese cuisine was served, and we had to eat with chopsticks and a bowl, and drink Chinese tea.

Cold drinks and beer were banned from the dining-table, and only allowed on weekdays, when we had a mixture of Portuguese and Chinese food. And so Sunday lunch had become a very special social occasion, when our family of three generations gathered together for a meal cooked and savoured at a leisurely pace, and sprinkled with the patriarch's reminiscences over the bad old days back in China and Beira. My married sister Sofia, her husband and four children also participated, for Sofia's husband had, over the years, become more a member of my family than his own, much to his mother's chagrin. As my father story-told his grandchildren about his early struggles, he reminded the older grandchildren not to take their present hunger-free days for granted, and to work hard at school. The world, he said, was fast changing, and in it there was no longer room for men like himself who, in the old world, could carve out a place for themselves by sheer hard work, guts, thrift, and luck. "You will need professional qualifications and knowledge to survive, wherever you go," he told his male grandchildren, and to his female grandchildren he added, "In this fast-changing world, women too are going to work and compete with men for jobs. Aim high and don't settle for a domestic life."

Isabel was five years my senior and working at the time as a book-keeper for a Chinese businessman who had a clothes factory in Beira. He was born in Macao, but he and his family moved to Beira where he married a local Chinese girl. He was truly a mandarin for, unlike my father's generation who were originally poor peasants from Southern China but who eventually prospered in Mozambique, his family had brought with them capital from Macao and invested it locally. He was self-confident and abrasive, and a lover of brothels and high-stake gambling. He commuted frequently to the Far East, and rumour had it that he was involved in drug trafficking, bringing into the country heroin and marijuana, which he then distributed to his connections in Southern Rhodesia and South Africa. It was also rumoured that it was this shady side of his business which financed his factory and store in Beira, as well as his gambling extravagances and whores. The authorities were suspicious about his business transactions, but were unable to nail down concrete evidence to justify the rumours, for high officials in every relevant sector were bribed into silence.

Isabel enjoyed working for her employer, now known as Senhor Mário, because it was easier for his predominantly European clientele to call him by a Portuguese name. As his surname was Mah, it was unanimously decided that he should adopt the name Mário, which sounded simple but stylish, and suited his flamboyant image. Isabel found Senhor Mário kind and generous to his employees, at least those she came into contact with, who were Portuguese and Chinese. He paid well and offered a generous scheme of occupational welfare; and not many local business enterprises could be said to be so benevolently inclined, Isabel said.

Senhor Mário boasted to anyone who cared to listen that he lusted after women, particularly those with an "atomic bomb", as he called it. Chinese women, he claimed, lacked boobs, and that was why, he confided, he seldom touched his wife who, in spite of her mother's advice that the surest way to keep her husband in bed was to sleep naked, failed to hold him down. So Senhor Mário frequented brothels and hired Portuguese and mulatto women.

There existed at the time a distribution process of prostitutes throughout the country, whereby the most beautiful ones went to the capital city, the less beautiful ones to Beira, and the uglier ones to the cities in the north. At the peak of Senhor Mário's sexual prowess, there lived in Lourenço Marques a highly desirable, elite courtesan called Candida who, according to the legend of the day, knew exactly how to satisfy every male sexual whim, and commanded such a high fee for her services that it was calculated that in no time at all she would be able to retire and retreat to a secure future in Portugal. Not only was she young, but she didn't plaster her face with layers and layers of cosmetics as most in her profession did, so that she looked clean and fresh to her prospective clients. Senhor Mário, having satiated himself on lean and fat flesh alike at every brothel in town, got bored. He turned his eyes in the direction of Lourenço Marques, packed his wife and children off to Salisbury to stay with friends, and had Candida flown to Beira for a weekend of sexual orgy in his house. He paid her twenty-five thousand *escudos*, and she engaged him in every athletic feat and magic trick prescribed in the sex manuals. In fact, she exercised him so hard that after that weekend, he began to have recurring nightmares.

Every night, he dreamt he was galloping in a field so hard and fast that his goose-pimpled testicles inflated into two giant balloons and lifted him off his mare, carrying him up into the sky over the River Rovuma. An eagle flew by, flapped its wings, and in full swoop, plummeted towards the balloons and pricked them. They burst with a loud pop, and Senhor Mário rocketed downwards into the river and drowned. Waking startled and bathed in sweat, he hurried to an Indian fortune-teller, who had a practice in Esturro, and asked for the meaning of his recurring nightmare. But the fortune-teller couldn't provide him with a satisfactory explanation, so he went to see a black witchdoctor, wondering whether an enemy had perhaps cast a curse on him. But the witchdoctor's findings were negative. And the same nightmare plagued him until 1975.

After the official declaration of Independence in June 1975, Senhor Mário's family went back to Macao. He stayed behind in Beira to wind down his business affairs and clear his belongings before joining his family in the Far East. One uneventful afternoon, Senhor Mário was walking down Bougainvillea Avenue at a leisurely pace, when a car pulled up at his side. Two faces stared at him, and one of them said, "You there, come over here," as the figure of a tall African in uniform stepped out of the car. In previous years, Senhor Mário would have been outraged by the insolent manner in which he was now being addressed by the two FRELIMO soldiers, and would have taken them to task with the Portuguese authorities. But things had changed. The boot was on the other foot. Towering over Senhor Mário, the soldier said, "Your identity card." Senhor Mário fumbled in the pockets of his pink spotted shirt and his burgundy corduroy trousers. "I haven't got it on me. I must have left it at home," he said meekly. "That's the excuse you people give when we catch you out. Come on, get in the car." The soldier jerked his head in the direction of the car. Senhor Mário thought of running away, because he had heard rumours that anyone found without an identity card would either be sent away to one of FRELIMO's re-education camps or to jail. But where could he run to? he asked himself. And so, resigned, he climbed into the back seat of the car.

The car proceeded down the avenue, past the Praça do Município, rounded the corner of a jewellery shop, and halted in front of a police station. Senhor Mário got scared and felt every drop of fear ooze out through the pores of his skin. One of the soldiers got out of the car, opened the back door, and beckoned him to step out. Inside the police station, Senhor Mário was told to fill in a form, giving details of his date of birth, profession, and home address. Half an hour later, he was led into a bare, whitewashed little square room, with a rectangular table and two chairs. A policeman stood by the window, faceless and impassive. Senhor Mário was told to sit down, and an officer in plain clothes began to interrogate him, pacing up and down the room. Why was he without an identity card? Where was he going at the time he was picked up in the avenue? Senhor Mário tried to answer in a straightforward manner, saying he had left his card at home, at which his interrogator pounced on him, reminding him of FRELIMO's regulations that every Mozambican, black or white, resident or citizen, had to carry with him his identity card at all times. Senhor Mário clenched his fists under the table, trying fiercely to control his indignation and racial prejudice, muttering to himself in Chinese, "You black bastard, I would have smashed your face before June 25th for daring to treat a whiter man than yourself like this." But with a tremendous effort, he calmed down. When asked about his destination at the time of his arrest, he answered that he was going to the post office to pick up his mail from his box. All of a sudden, two black men entered the room, walked up to where the interrogator was standing, and whispered something in his ear. With their backs turned to Senhor Mário, the three men sniggered. Senhor Mário tried in vain to make out what they were saying. Then, to his surprise, he saw the three men turn towards him smiling broadly, baring their teeth at him. The interrogator sat in a chair for the first time, while the other two sat on the table, their legs dangling. "You certainly are who you say you are," remarked the interrogator, and after a long, calculated pause, he pointed to the papers that the other two men had just brought in, and said: "Well, well, the legendary Senhor Mário himself! Your decadent, playboy lifestyle is well known among us. Of course, you know by now what FRELIMO's stand on sexual exploitation is, and you are aware what the penalty is for anyone who exploits women for personal pleasure and treats them purely as commodity objects. We are going to shut down all nightclubs and casinos, purge this city of its prostitution venues, and re-educate people morally. So we are going to send you to one of our re-education camps up in the north, where instead of fucking so hard, you'll work hard. We will assess your progress, and if you prove sufficiently self-critical over your past behaviour, we'll review your position and perhaps allow you back to Beira."

Just my luck to be picked up like this, as I'm about to leave the country, Senhor Mário cursed himself, and he felt salty tears pricking his eyes. He wanted to cry aloud, but held back his tears in shame as he was led away from the room.

On the morning of his first day at the re-education camp, Senhor Mário was sent by the Commune's Council to weed in a hot, dusty field near the River Rovuma. As he crouched and plucked out a weed, he buried his head in his chest and gazed at his innermost soul, tucked safely away under his shapeless baggy trousers, and realised for the first time what the recurring nightmare which had haunted him for over a decade meant. He felt castrated in the wilderness, and for the first time in his adult life, he wept unashamedly. And the story of Senhor Mário's moral repentance in the re-education camp became part of local folklore. When he was released and finally joined his family in Macao, Senhor Mário became a recluse and led the life of a monk.

Isabel was in a buoyant mood when she called at our house. As soon as she got into her car, she announced, "Alfredo has asked me to marry him, and I've accepted."

"I'm so happy for you! When is he leaving the army?"

"In four months' time, but he'll be down for the weekend in a fortnight's time. His commander in Nampula has granted him a short leave, and we'll be officially engaged then. Needless to say, you'll be one of my bridesmaids."

"Oh, I'd love that!"

"We won't be living here in Beira after we have married."

"Really? Where will you be going? Does Alfredo want to go back to Portugal?"

"No. We'll be emigrating to Brazil. Alfredo's uncle has a small business enterprise of his own in São Paulo which, among other things, makes sunglasses. He has no children of his own, and he would like Alfredo to go and work with him. He has offered Alfredo a managerial traineeship to begin with. My parents have agreed to our marriage. And in many ways, I am glad to start a new life in a new country."

"Yes," I muttered quietly.

Isabel's hands were resting on the steering-wheel of her car, and as she remarked that she was glad to start a new life elsewhere, she gazed ahead of her, oblivious to my company, her mind buried in dark thoughts of her past. I gently squeezed her left hand, but she didn't respond.

I recalled that fateful afternoon five years ago, when she climbed the steps of the Chinese Association on her father's arm, on her wedding day. It was a clear blue April day, and the band had just begun to play the Wedding March. All the guests were seated in the large hall, and the bridegroom, Henrique, and his two best men were standing in their allocated places at the far end of the hall, waiting to be summoned by the master of ceremonies to walk up the aisle, preceding the bridal train by a few yards. Suddenly, Isabel was literally paralysed. A strong, persistent whirlwind trapped her steps, rooting her firmly to the steps. Her father and the bridesmaids tried to pull her free from the unexpected ambush, but a sudden gust of wind slapped them away from the bride, and Isabel's father rolled down the steps. An invisible hand snatched Isabel's wedding veil and bouquet from her, and she fainted. The bridegroom darted forward to rescue his damsel, but another gust of wind smashed the windows nearby, and the flying glass cut the bridegroom in the face. He lurched forward, burying his face in his hands, blood running down his lapel. The guests gasped in horror, and the music stopped playing. The master of ceremonies announced through the microphone: "Ladies and gentlemen, please remain calm. We are sorry we have to postpone the wedding ceremony. Please leave quietly and in peace. Thank you." The guests filed out of the hall in silence, stunned by the chilling atmosphere surrounding them.

When the bride came round in the reassuring surroundings of her own home, she said in a matter-of-fact way to her mother, "João wouldn't let me into the hall." Her mother, sitting by her bedside, dabbed her burning forehead with an ice-filled rubber bottle, and shushed her, saying, "Don't tire yourself now, my daughter, have some rest. Later, we'll talk."

That evening, Pearl and her husband convened a meeting of the eldest members of the Chinese community in their house. Pearl asked the sages for their guidance on how to deal with the tragic event of the day, and recounted her daughter's version of the tragedy.

The oldest man among the sages, a silver-haired octogenarian, began by explaining, "João and Isabel had a long-standing and loving relationship spanning many years. They were childhood fiancés. It is inevitable that when he died from leukaemia, he wouldn't let go of her. Do you all remember how, tortured by João's slow, painful death, Isabel slipped onto João's finger the ring she was wearing, in order to comfort him in his last moments? Long before he actually died, she was virtually his widow, and when he breathed his last, he took with him the memory of her as his own wife. That is why he now refuses to give her up to someone else in marriage. What I propose you should do now, as Isabel's parents, is to try and placate, to pacify João's lonely, aggrieved soul, by holding a reconciliation ceremony for him, and praying to his spirit to let go of Isabel and bless her marriage to Henrique."

"Yes, we agree," said the other sages in unison. "It is a great pity we had not remembered to warn you of the need to appease João's spirit first, before Isabel's wedding this afternoon. But it is still not too late, and you must carry out the reconciliation ceremony soon, without too much delay."

Pearl and her husband chose a Sunday morning, and preparations were set for the ceremonial ritual. On the appointed day, in a ritual performed and witnessed only by the Chinese elders, offerings were made to the dead soul amid a feast of poached duck, chicken and pork, rice, wine, incense sticks, and much chanting and mumbling. After the reconciliation ceremony, the elders and Isabel went to the cemetery and placed a bouquet of white chrysanthemums at João's tomb. They burnt incense sticks by his tomb and prayed. Before they left, they kow-towed three times in front of João's tomb as a mark of respect for his soul. When the elders reached the cemetery's exit gate, they turned round instinctively and thought they saw the silhouette of a young man wave to them in the far distance.

Isabel took years to recover from the incident, by which time Henrique's parents had changed their minds and thought it bad luck for their son to marry Isabel. With discretion and grace, both parties went their own way. A year later, Isabel went to Lourenço Marques for a holiday, and there she met a Portuguese soldier named Alfredo, who was at the time stationed in the capital. Theirs was a meeting of souls, and although he was later transferred to Nampula in the north, they wrote regularly, and saw each other as often as possible. And now Isabel was about to embark on a new life in a new country, and with this new man.

She heaved a deep sigh of relief, and turning her eyes in my direction, said, smiling, "For a moment, morbid thoughts got the better of me. What an unpromising way to start a new life, wouldn't you say?" She fired the engine, and away we drove to Macuti Beach for my rendezvous. As I hopped out of the car, Isabel reminded me of the hour she had to collect me from the beach. "You have precisely three hours. Be here promptly when I come back to pick you up, won't you?" she said.

I nodded and waved, took off my shoes, and ran across the warm silver sand, past the lighthouse, until I reached the old shipwreck, half buried in the wet sand.

Chico was by the shipwreck, scribbling on the sand with a piece of driftwood. We had both come to say goodbye to each other and didn't know how. I knelt by his side, and he took my hands in his. Chico began by saying, "I'll be back for you when I've completed my studies..." I shook my head, interrupting him, and said, "Let's not think or talk of tomorrow, Chico. We are here together, and that is the important thing. Tomorrow may not exist for us. Africa may not exist for us tomorrow. God knows where we will all be tomorrow. I will always love you, Chico, but I won't always be in love with you. For me to acknowledge this now is my way of saying I have grown up. Let us be grateful for this moment alone. And if we are to part forever, we know we will have lost, not through lack of faith and optimism, but against history, against the storms of history that are now roaring southwards, and will drown us all one day."

"I have loved you since I first met you," said Chico, "when you were only a skinny eleven-year-old with large expressive eyes and a ponytail, and I a pimply sixteen-year-old. Do you remember?"

Yes, I did. I was playing basketball with friends at the Chinese School's basketball pitch. I had flung the ball too hard, and it flew off the court and hit a passer-by. I ran after the ball. The stranger, hit on the head, picked up the ball and held it tight in his hands, not budging from where he was standing. I held out my arms, expecting him to throw it back to me, but he remained motionless. I walked up to him and asked, "Could you please pass me back my ball?" But he only answered, "What is your name?" I thought he was being cheeky, and had in mind not to reply, but as I wanted the ball back quickly, I obliged him. "Estrela. And what is yours?" He smiled a grown-up smile and said, "Chico," and threw the ball back to me.

I did not see my stranger again until I was a teenager and he a medical student. By this time, he was no longer a pimply boy, but a tall, handsome athlete. He was a stranger to me because he had lived most of his life in Southern Rhodesia. When his parents split up, he was only a child. He and his mother moved to Salisbury to live with an uncle, who provided his childhood with a father figure, and who eventually became a *de facto* father, mentor, and patron. When he was sixteen years old, his mother decided to return to Beira to live with her sister, but Chico remained in Salisbury to continue with his education. He visited his mother during the school holidays, and when he started university, he saw more of her because of his now longer holidays. It was during one of these holidays that we ran into each other again, for the second time, at a New Year's party at the Chinese School. We recognised each other instantly in spite of the passing years. We danced the whole party together, and soon began to see a lot of each other during his holidays in Beira. We enjoyed each other's company, sang and danced together. Chico came to my house with his guitar, and sang and imitated Elvis Presley. We borrowed books and records from each other, and I practised the English I learnt at school with him. We wrote to each other regularly over the years, and on a few occasions, I went up to Salisbury to see him and go with him to special concerts, to hear Sachmo, Cliff Richard, and Helen Shapiro.

Soon my father's displeasure at my dating Chico became plainly visible. Whenever Chico called at the house, he paced up and down outside the sitting-room, hinting to Chico that he was unwelcome in his house. When Chico's letters arrived, my father threw them to the floor, in my presence. It wounded Chico that the patriarch should disrespect him solely because of his parents' divorce and his mother's involvement with a married mulatto. And in a subconscious way, Chico's loyalty and dedication to me became almost an obsession, a determined demonstration on his part of his ability to love and honour a commitment, in spite of his parents' failings. He often spoke of marrying me as soon as he completed his medical studies and residency, and vowed that ours would be a happy and fruitful union, unlike that of his parents.

If my father was brutally frank in his feelings towards a possible union between Chico and me, so was his mother. But his aunt liked me and welcomed me in her house. "You must not mind my sister," Chico's aunt said, "she is very possessive over her only son, her precious doctor." But Chico's aunt was no ordinary woman. It was rumoured that she menstruated for three weeks out of four in the month, and that her husband was then spotted sneaking off in the early morning to another woman's bed. This other woman was known in town as Madame Rosa, and her cuckold of a husband got out of her bed every morning at two o'clock during those three weeks in order to allow Chico's uncle to crawl into it. This *ménage à trois* and Madame Rosa's boudoir charms brought her a small fortune, and in no time at all, she built a comfortable house for herself, opened a supermarket of her own, and sent her son to study abroad. Chico's uncle, on the other hand, remained an impecunious shopkeeper for the rest of his days. And Chico's aunt's unusual periods were only an excuse she invented to repel her husband from her side.

"I will always love you," repeated Chico, "and wherever we may be, I will find you. The war will blow over, you'll see, and it will not separate us!" I did not protest. We were in love and alive, and I did not wish to think of tomorrow. For when you are young, you are so idealistic that you begin to sound sentimental.

And between the gentle sound and rhythm of the folding and unfolding of one wave and the next, the gift of loving was exchanged with tenderness.

9

THE CLAY MASK

We seldom talked about politics in our household, least of all Mozambican politics. It was as if faceless eyes spied on us, and sharp ears eavesdropped from every corner of the house, and phantasmagorical shadows lurked behind doors and swished past along the corridors. Eyes and ears and shadows slotted into place in a shapeless, anonymous, masked intelligence, and haunted every breath we drew.

My parents and relatives and friends had sailed many a tempestuous sea in search of a living in a new country, and having arrived at their destination, wanted only to settle down and get on with the practicalities of their day-to-day life. Poor immigrants, they had no will nor the capacity to concern themselves with the refinements of intellectual questioning of their new and foreign world. Hungry, they settled for little. A bowl of rice, a roof over their head, personal endurance, and a burning spur to thrust forward and make the best of what they had, there and then, these were the basic ingredients of their daily philosophical diet. For this was the bare essence of their survival. So they chose to live and let live and, chameleon-like, they traipsed their way through the dense bush. After all, it didn't behove the likes of settler immigrants to query the righteousness and expediency of policies dictated by the iron grip of the Portuguese Master. Didn't he know all the answers? Didn't he know all there was to know?

One day, the Portuguese Master made a white clay mask in his own image and baked it in the tropical heat. He abandoned it in the scorching sun, and the clay began to get tanned and tinged with different hues – yellow, light brown, dark brown, and charcoal. Gradually, after forty-two years' exposure in the sun, the clay mask turned black. And its Caucasian features were lost.

When the Chinese chameleons reached a wide clearing in the bush, they saw the black mask hoisted up on a wooden pole, and they didn't like it. For the first time during all their years in the African wilderness, they reacted and condemned the metamorphosis of the white mask in outright terms, and fled *en masse* from the green swampy land. The extremely old and weary, who had no families to help them in the long march out of the bush, had no alternative but to remain in it. Two spinster sisters, having no men or friends to comfort them in the hazardous search for a new home away from the bush, chose to stay. Here in the bush, they reflected, they knew their bearings at least. And a handful of able-bodied young men who had *machambas* felt they could adapt to the new political regime and survive. They stayed, but advised their women and children to leave with their relatives on the long journey to the unknown, for their own physical safety. For the

Chinese reasoned that five hundred years of colonial exploitation, gold, slavery, and ivory, would not pass without explosions of random revenge killings, butchery, and rape. And although FRELIMO's declared philosophy was non-racist, they could not help fearing for the safety of their wives and children, and wishing to avoid trouble, took no chances. The ghost of Amin's handling of Asians in Uganda after independence haunted the Chinese in Mozambique. This, together with their rejection of socialism in principle, combined with a large dose of racial prejudice against the reliability of an African government, finally determined their decision to kick themselves out of Mozambique.

And so on a July evening in 1975, my family of three generations of uprooted Mozambicans boarded a Portuguese airliner and fled to Portugal to place themselves at the mercy of dispersal agencies. Nomads of survival, we were now flying from our African purgatory to the concrete jungle, to whichever country was willing to accept us.

I could not read my father's thoughts as we fastened our seatbelts inside the plane. His face was expressionless, but I could sense the calm pain in his heart. I felt he had been training himself to outfeel his pain, and in doing so, he found his strength of mind.

"Look, Father, we are taking off," I said. His eyes glistened with moisture, and with a quick, awkward turn of his head, he glanced back at the airport building which was now fast disappearing from view. The plane climbed up and up. Tears welled up in my father's eyes, and he sobbed out loud, burying his head in his freckled, wrinkled hands. I squeezed his thin forearm to comfort him and said, "Don't cry, Father. Nothing lasts forever. It was Africa. And Africa is for Africans. You are an accomplished and self-fulfilled man, and you have lived a full life. Think of the joy your story-telling of memories will bring to your grandchildren and great-grandchildren." He fumbled for a handkerchief in his trouser pocket, dried his tears and blew his nose.

"I am an old man now," he replied, "not the young man of forty-two years ago."

"I know, but we your children are young. And wherever we may end up, we will stay together. United, the Chinese way."

He said nothing. I understood then his fear of a future in which he had to depend entirely on the care and loyalty of his children. And I knew then the tragedy of being uprooted in old age. And in my father's case, uprooted for the second time in the seventy-five years of his existence.

"I am glad your mother is not alive to see this. She is at least spared this pain," my father said quietly.

The young *machambeiros* did survive after Independence, and one in particular thrived – my cousin Ferryboat, Uncle Knight's eldest son. A decade later, when small-scale private enterprises were once again allowed to operate in the new land of the black mask, Ferryboat prospered, and became known among locals as "our African mandarin". But unlike the former mandarins, who were fiercely anti-communist, Ferryboat found sanctuary among the communist Chinese at their embassy in the renamed capital city, Maputo. Outwardly, he was conforming in order to survive in the new era, just as his predecessors had in the old one. But unlike the former mandarins who had, over the years, become more like white Mozambicans, Ferryboat now clung, in his heart and mind, more and more to his Chinese identity.

But Ferryboat had always been a survivor, a compromiser, and an accommodator. As a youth, aware that his own father's prospects in life would never improve, he set out to marry into money. And when the opportunity arose, he found himself a rich bride in the person of a spinster, years older than himself, and daughter of a prosperous merchant in Lourenço Marques. As the bride's family were concerned that she might end up on the shelf were they to spurn humble Ferryboat's proposal, they accepted it. And they never regretted it, as their son-in-law proved to be a cooperative and helpful partner in the running of the family business.

Ferryboat's in-laws had started as humble *machambeiros* in Lourenço Marques. In their reminiscences of their past poverty, they would recount to anyone who listened their earlier experiences of deprivation, when they had to make an egg stretch among their four children at the dinner table. As with some Chinese, prosperity knocked on their door eventually, and they branched out into more lucrative forms of commerce. The family, however, retained the *machamba*, which went on yielding healthy profits. And in the years to come, history proved that theirs had been a wise decision. For after Independence in 1975, when private traders no longer had a viable existence in the new order, causing most Chinese to leave the country, Cousin Ferryboat found he could remain and survive as a *machambeiro*.

"Why start all over from scratch in a new, unknown country, maybe having to face unemployment and homelessness, when I can at least enjoy the security of a roof and the fruits of my plot of land here?" Ferryboat reflected. "Money and contacts in high places will speak here, in spite of FRELIMO's Marxist rhetoric. You cannot wipe out centuries of corruption and bribery overnight in a single revolution. No, I will stay put. But I will send my wife and two daughters away, to whichever country will take them. When the dust of the post-Independence chaos and instability has settled, I shall send for them, and we shall live together again. Meanwhile, I will work in the family's *machamba*, sell my quota to the state, and do what I like with the rest of my produce. I have good friends among the diplomats in the Chinese Embassy here, and as they are grateful for my reliable daily deliveries of fresh vegetables to the embassy staff, they'll help me to send a monthly allowance to my wife abroad. What are friends and contacts for? One good turn deserves another. Besides, we Chinese have to stick together now and help each other out."

Nine years after Independence, when President Samora Machel – desperate after three years of drought, a devastating flood, and an armed insurgency affecting much of the country – resolved to make a decisive

U-turn in economic policy and went out of his way to attract international investment and multi-national companies to its worn-out wealth and charms, Cousin Ferryboat wrote to his wife and asked her to return home with the children. It was too late. She and the children had by now made a new life for themselves, and had no wish to return to a country which they no longer considered their home. Cousin Ferryboat took up with a *mulata* and lived happily ever after in his *machamba*.

The two virgin spinster sisters who chose to remain were attacked and raped. The knife wounds inflicted on their faces were so deep and numerous that when they eventually healed, they became maps of rivers. And many a time, in the quiet of their solitary pain, the sisters wept over their fate. Their tears swelled and flooded the rivers on their maps.

10

BOUQUET OF CONCILIATION

8th July, 1984

Last night I dreamt I was back in Beira. At the cemetery. I had gone to put flowers on my mother's grave and couldn't find it in its usual place.

I walked through the stillness of the whitewashed enclosure with a bouquet of red carnations, but could not see my mother's name anywhere. It seemed hours before I reached the far end of the cemetery, where a towering wall of steel lockers glared down at me. I wondered what it was. Suddenly, I caught sight of my mother's name in a locker on the sixth row. I took one single carnation from the bouquet (they only sold red carnations at the florist) and knotted its light stem around the handle of my mother's locker. I then placed the whole bunch of flowers at the foot of the steel wall, in collective memory of all those buried there. I was just beginning to do things in a collective spirit. Perhaps there is still hope for me there.

END

OTHER STORIES

FACE REGAINED

In a small, cluttered backroom, soaked in clammy heat and facing onto a patch of dusty earth beyond which was a wire-enclosed vegetable garden, Violeta sat motionless at her sewing machine by the mesh window, her countenance dazed by pain. Large, rectangular sheets of multi-coloured cotton, which she had cut out to make *capulanas*, lay limply by her feet on the concrete floor. Even the urgent need to get the frayed edges of the cut-out sheets hemmed in and stitched in time to sell in her shop seemed lost to Violeta. A mosquito, bloated by multiple recent helpings of fresh human blood, drifted drunkenly into the room and hummed sluggishly round and round the porcelain deadness of Violeta's unchiselled face. Violeta did not react. A mosquito swatter dangled from a plastic-coated hook on the wall, plastered with garish calendars. Unwilling to let slip another opportunity to feast on submissive prey, the mosquito stopped circling in the humid air and dug into the flatness of Violeta's right eyelid. Violeta felt it swell and itch, and hood over her eye, blurring her vision. But she remained still, indifferent to her attacker's sharp, venomous sting. In the burning heat of the backyard, Violeta's five-year-old son teased and chased the family's Dalmatian guard-dog with a straw broom, and amid flirtatious yelps and shrieks of delight, dog and child wended their way into the vegetable garden.

Violeta wanted to scream and cry, but couldn't. Her eyes were parched, her mind exhausted, and her heart numb with pain. She had become the town bigamist's first wife. No, not his first wife; not even his wife, Violeta mused with shame. She had in fact become an unmarried mother, in spite of sixteen years of marriage to a Chinaman, from whom she had borne four strong, healthy children. For her marriage certificate, issued, signed, and witnessed by the town's appointed Marriage Committee, elected among the most respected elders from the members of the Chinese Association, had now been dismissed as invalid – not only by her faithless husband, but more importantly by the mighty law of the land. Today, at this dead hour, her bigamist husband was gloating over his honeymoon on Paradise Island with a new bride, after a triumphant wedding at the Catholic Cathedral in the capital city, Lourenço Marques.

"Why should I be left, an unmarried mother, just because of a piece of paper?" Violeta questioned with frozen anger. "When I got married, I accepted my marriage certificate, vows, and wedding ceremony at the Chinese School as valid and binding, on faith and trust, like all Chinese men and women before me had done. I didn't know it was necessary to go to the Portuguese Registry Office, too. That's something the younger generation have learned. How was I to foresee that my husband, who loved me when we married, should one day dishonour and pronounce our marriage as invalid in order to marry someone else and disclaim any obligation towards our children? Worst of all, that in the eyes of the Portuguese law, my marriage would only be a private ritual, performed and witnessed by a group of appointed marriage-makers who had no authority to legalise a marriage in the first place?"

Broken lines furrowed across Violeta's forehead, and her small eyes tightened in a contortion of repressed pain from the depths of her shame. She felt ashamed and humiliated by the cursory manner in which her husband, Romeu, had dismissed her.

On the morning Romeu left her and the children permanently, he gripped her by her skinny arm and dragged her to the dressing table in their bedroom, and spat out with contempt, "Look at yourself in the mirror! A dried-up old woman, sleepwalking through life as a dutiful and virtuous wife. Do you want to hear what *she* is like? A woman who dares! A whore in bed, and a companion and friend out of it."

"How dare you speak to me like this," retorted Violeta in a wounded, but quiet and dignified voice, wrestling her arm free with a forceful push. "Six years ago, I would have put up with your insults meekly and silently. But not now! A lover, a companion, and a friend indeed – have I not been these things to you when you still wanted me? Am I to blame if we only see each other once every six months?" Raising her voice and wagging her forefinger at him, Violeta wailed, "I work my guts out here, looking after this miserable shop, the children, and your elderly uncle, while you live and work in Govuro, and come home to visit us only twice a year. You still remember, don't you, or have you conveniently forgotten, why the children and I had to remain in Beira instead of going to live in Govuro with you?"

"The children have to go to school, and there are no schools in Govuro!" Romeu chanted and mocked, putting on his wife's voice, and then added, "No, I have not forgotten. Bah! How you bore me! Jesus! I am sick of you and the children!"

"If you really wanted me as a wife, friend, and companion," nagged Violeta, "you would have come back home to live with us and work in the shop. Instead, you chose to go to Louenço Marques every weekend to see your whore and—"

"Don't call her names," Romeu interrupted her. "I am going to marry her."

"Marry her? Over my dead body! I won't give you a divorce!"

"You won't give me a divorce?" Romeu scoffed, and then added condescendingly, "That's a joke, coming from you. My dear, a divorce is not yours to give. As far as I and the Portuguese law are concerned, you and I are not married. Never have been married. That piece of paper, that marriage certificate issued by a bunch of idiots sixteen years ago, is worth nothing. And I owe you and the children nothing. Do you hear me? Nothing! Legally speaking, the children are bastards, not my children. And don't you try to fight me, because I have the law on my side. You'll only be fighting a losing battle. So don't expect any money for the children from me, because from this very minute, I wash my hands of you." Romeu brushed his hands as he spoke the last words, walked out of the room, and left the house without saying goodbye to his uncle or children. That was the last Violeta saw of her husband.

Accompanied by her grey-haired father, Violeta trundled her truck down bumpy roads to the town centre to consult a lawyer, and pleaded against all odds for him to defend her case in the Portuguese court. After a quick glance at Violeta's marriage certificate, the lawyer shook his head and explained in the least complicated manner he could think of, "I really am sorry. Much as I sympathise with your case, I have to be blunt and admit it is a lost cause. Your marriage certificate won't hold up in court. You see, we live in a country governed by Portugal, and the Portuguese law, as it stands, requires that when two people get married, they do it according to certain well-established rules. This is to say, they either get married at the registry office with the required number of witnesses, or in the church. The Chinese wedding you had would only be regarded as a private arrangement, not a legal marriage. Even if I agreed to take on your case, it would be a long, protracted legal battle and might take years before the court reached a decision, by which time your husband would have married his woman anyway, and you would have incurred high expenses in legal fees. Fees you could hardly afford, given your present circumstances. I would advise you to keep whatever resources you have left for the children. You see, the chances of my winning the case for you, if I took it up, would be very remote indeed. I am so sorry, madam."

"*Senhor advogado*," cried Violeta's father, shamed by his son-in-law's dishonourable treatment of his only child, "we are willing to spend whatever is necessary on fees. Even if we have to borrow the money or raise it among our compatriots. I am a retired teacher, but I run a small shop now, and although we haven't much money, we'll manage the fees. Please, help us!"

"Why don't you think it over, and come back and see me another day?" suggested the lawyer, who felt sorry for the wiry old man's abundant tears, and hadn't the heart to repeat how hopeless Violeta's case was.

Violeta knew that neither she nor her father would be returning to the lawyer's office. She felt no self-pity, only anger. She also knew, there and then, that she would have to take the law into her own hands and avenge the shame, dishonour, and suffering she and her children were undergoing. Exactly how she would do this, she wasn't sure. At least, not yet. But in time, she believed, she would think up an effective way of punishing Romeu. She imagined how she could go to a witchdoctor and ask him to put a curse on the husband, and on the husband's wedding day itself, send her children to the capital city to pinch, kick, and verbally assault their father when he stood at the altar at his new bride's side, to accuse him of bigamy and shame him in the presence of the invited congregation.

Violeta recollected with sadness her seventeenth birthday, when she married as soon as she completed her six years of primary education at the Chinese School, where her father was a teacher. In that year, a young Chinaman, with pouting sensual lips, who had come to Beira to live with a widowed, childless uncle after he had become an orphan during the Sino-Japanese War in 1937, proposed to her through a go-between. He had spent two years coveting her from a distance, as she arrived and left the school building every day in the safe company of her father. Romeu prowled around the entrance gate of the school for a brief glimpse of the trim and delicate-looking Violeta, in her blue and white school uniform, white ankle socks, and Alice hairband. On wet days, he sat behind the steering wheel of his lorry, parked right in front of the school, and Violeta could feel the fire of his burning stare crackle out, "That is the girl I want!" Although she was apprehensive, almost afraid of the predatory quality of his interest in her, she was nevertheless flattered by his unflagging interest, as he waited for her arrival and departure from school, every day during term time, come rain or sun, over two full years. So, in spite of her tender age, and unsure of her feelings towards her persistent twenty-five-year-old suitor, Violeta accepted his marriage proposal, with her parents' consent and encouragement. After all, she asked herself, didn't most of her contemporaries aspire to get married at an early age, and to the first suitor who came along with reasonable credentials? If she let this opportunity of getting married pass, would she get another chance? Her suitor's uncle, a Taoist and a friend of her parents, was known to be a kind man, and as he was a widower, she wouldn't have to put up with a mother-in-law. True, Violeta told herself, she wouldn't be marrying into a well-to-do family, and she would have to work very hard at Romeu's uncle's shop in Manga, but then the majority of girls of her age married shopkeepers, so she couldn't really complain, she reasoned.

On her wedding day. Violeta wore a long, white organza dress, with fresh white flowers stitched onto her wide full skirt. And at a ceremony at the Wedding Hall of the Chinese School, attended by most of the Chinese population in Beira, she and her husband signed their marriage certificate and kow-towed three times to the elected Marriage Committee, who stood with stern faces under a gigantic, framed photograph of Dr Sun Yat-Sen, hung from a wooden beam on the high ceiling. They danced to the music played by a band of semi-toothless Goan and Chinese musicians, and ate and drank merrily with the guests. Children, not content with guzzling down European cakes at the party itself, snapped up chocolate éclairs and cream-filled pastries, and wrapped them with their handkerchiefs into knotted bundles to take home. Under a shower of multi-coloured confetti, the newly-weds tunnelled their way out of the Wedding Hall to a new beginning together.

At first, love was abundant. Violeta, good at sewing, made dresses and *capulanas*, and sold them in her shop to native women. Romeu racked his brains for ways to increase the meagre profits derived from their small general store. The Taoist uncle, now retired and in his sixties, was busily involved in transcendental meditation and the martial arts. Having acquired a niece-in-law to look after him, or better still to slave for him, he now began to develop new habits on a whim. He rejected what he called chemically-treated piped water and insisted instead on drinking only water from the old well, which was situated a quarter of a mile away from the back of the shop house, on the pretext that drinking fresh, natural water from a well contributed to healthy longevity. Violeta resented this extra and unnecessary chore, as she was the one who had to draw water from the well every day and lug it home in a bucket made from a large old tin, and she saw no logic or benefit in the old man's insistence on drinking water from the well since she still had to boil it all the same. Nevertheless, she carried out her chores dutifully, and outwardly uncomplaining. With the passing of the years, she came to realise that her life was but a series of duties she had to perform. Duties as a co-breadwinner and housewife, wife, mother, and daughter-in-law. Was this the fate of all Chinese daughters? She often complained to herself. It shouldn't be, she answered herself, and rebelled in thought against her fate, but with each rising dawn, she got up and performed her duties mechanically. "Someone has to do it," she explained to herself, as she shuffled onto the arid expanse of earth which rolled out under her heavy feet, to fetch water from the well.

Within the first five years of her marriage, three children tumbled out of Violeta's thin but strong body. The arrival of her first-born saw the materialisation of a well planned-out vegetable garden, whose home-grown produce not only cut down food bills, but also satisfied the uncle's newly acquired fastidiousness over fresh food. Now, different soups had to be freshly made for lunch and dinner separately, and orange juice had to be consumed within the three minutes after it had been squeezed. Thus Violeta found herself at the beck and call of Romeu's uncle, and at the mercy of his excessive demands.

As their shop still made very marginal profits, Romeu studied seriously the possibility of moving into a different area of business. But it took him five years from the day his third son was born, to raise enough capital and find a business partner to launch a small fish-salting enterprise in Govuro, further south in the country and nearer the capital city. Violeta, they both agreed, would continue running the shop in Beira, as the children had to go to school, and there were no schools at the time in Govuro. Romeu would visit his family as often as was practical, given the cost of travelling between the two places. During his first year away from home, Romeu missed his wife and travelled by helicopter to see her and the children once a month. Their first reunion was passionate and spontaneously loving, and as a result, their unplanned fourth son was born ten months later, after a long gap of seven years between the newborn and their third child. But gradually, Romeu got used to Violeta's absence, and his monthly visits to his family became more and more irregular. Often, he and his business partner sent for Portuguese prostitutes from the capital to entertain them in Govuro. And one fateful weekend, Romeu decided instead to truck down to Lourenço Marques himself for a short holiday alone. There, through a mutual acquaintance, he was introduced to a Chinese Mozambican in her early thirties, who impressed him as unusually self-confident. Margarida was, he reckoned, someone who knew exactly what she wanted, and wasn't afraid of reaching out and getting it. Because she seemed so different from shy and self-effacing Violeta, Romeu felt extremely attracted to her, and in no time they began an affair.

"You needn't go back to Govuro and work in that dump, Romeu! Anything to do with fishing makes one's hands and body smell so unpleasant!" And she laughed coquettishly. "Come and live in Lourenço Marques. My father will set you up in business. I mean business for a white market. None of that wretched shopkeeping for Blacks!" Margarida stated in a matter-of-fact manner. After a short pause, she dipped her well made-up eyes searchingly into Romeu's soul, and with a mascara-laden stare, ordered clearly, "And no more whores from now on. You don't need them, because you have me now. You must divorce your wife, Romeu, and marry me," she added.

"I have to work in Govuro for a while yet, at least until I've sold my share of the business. But I'll continue visiting you every weekend, or every other weekend."

"Oh! That won't do!" Margarida exclaimed. "If you can't come and live in Lourenço Marques yet, then I'm going to live with you in Govuro. As a wife. Don't protest, because I want to. And will."

Romeu felt uneasy about Margarida's forwardness. But flattered and intrigued by her determination to hunt him until she captured him, he succumbed to her well-packaged proposition. Romeu now entered into the habit of seeing his wife only twice a year, and when Margarida announced that she was pregnant, he knew only too well that the time had come for him to make good his promise of marrying her. He was aware he could dismiss Violeta without ceremony.

* * *

Violeta's eldest son, António, tapped the door gently and entered the room. He placed a glass of tea on the sewing machine, and said: "I brought some tea, Mother. Drink it while it's warm. Please, Mother!" Violeta lifted her empty glare towards her fifteen-year-old son, and for the first time that day broke out in tears. "My son, my poor boys," she said repeatedly. Her son bent down and crouched beside her. Resting a reassuring hand on her lap, he confided, "Don't pity your sons, Mother. Your boys are men now. You and I are going to Lourenço Marques to give Father a wedding present when he has returned from his honeymoon. We have a lot of work and planning to do between now and then. We'll give Father something he would never have expected from us. We'll perform the greatest act this town has ever known in its history, and people will applaud our ingenuity and talent. Cry and let it all out now, Mother, but don't mourn over the years you've wasted on a man like Father."

Violeta took the glass of tea her son now held out to her, and as she sipped the warm, comforting liquid, her tearful, swollen eyes plunged, hypnotised, into the glistening pools of her son's dilated eyes. Blistering sunbeams filtered through the wide mesh window into the room. Hatred sparkled diamonds of every colour and shape on moist retinas. Mother and son exchanged a conspiratorial smile. Shame knotted their grievous souls together.

*   *   *

Romeu was serving a client with his usual fixed grin, at the counter of his smart new shop. A tray of green jade figurines sat between him and his fussy customer who, in spite of his solicitous suggestions, couldn't make up her mind as to which of the figurines she wanted to buy. Her eyes darted restlessly from one object to another while she spoke with expansive gesticulations. Catching sight of an exquisitely carved camphor trunk in the far corner of the shop, she moved away from the counter, ignoring Romeu, who listened attentively to her chatter. The telephone rang. Romeu picked up the receiver, relieved to be momentarily rid of this tiresome customer. His wife Margarida was at the other counter, at that precise moment selling a copious amount of imported Chinese silk shirts to a Portuguese captain's wife.

"Yes, Romeu speaking. Who is that? Father Paulo? What a pleasant surprise! What can I do for you, Father?" Romeu asked.

"I'd like to see you today about some documents concerning your marriage," answered the voice at the other end of the line.

"Documents concerning my marriage?" Romeu stuttered, confused and worried. "Is there anything wrong with my marriage documents?" he brought himself to ask, gulping down a good dose of his own saliva.

"Not really," answered the priest, in a matter-of-fact tone of voice. "There are just a few points we seem to have overlooked when we issued your documents. Nothing too serious, but important enough for us to have to rectify them at once. Could you pop over within the next half an hour?"

"Well... I'm not sure... I am rather busy in the shop..."

"Your wife is there, isn't she? This won't take more than ten minutes, I assure you, and it's urgent."

"Well... if it's urgent, Father..."

"It is! I'll see you in the chapel in half-an-hour." And Father Paulo hung up.

Romeu hurried to his wife's side and told her about the phone call from their parish church. "I can't think what could possibly be wrong with our marriage papers," he said. "Do you think Violeta has complained to the church authorities?"

"What? That little mouse of a wife of yours? Nonsense!" Margarida scoffed. "It is probably some birth certificate we've forgotten to enclose with the various documents we submitted. Go. I'll be all right here in the shop."

Romeu entered the silence of the small parish church and made his way to the chapel. It was deserted. A tiny figure, clad and veiled in black, was praying with a rosary in the front pew. Father Paulo had said he would meet him there in the chapel. Romeu checked his wristwatch – no, he wasn't too early for the meeting. Father Paulo was probably in the sacristy, thought

Romeu, and he strode up the aisle past the woman in black. As he veered right towards the sacristy, he heard the entrance door of the chapel bang shut, and the iron bolt fall with a loud clank. Ah, it's Father Paulo, thought Romeu. He turned round, but to his astonishment saw his eldest son amble up the aisle towards him. So the boy had actually come to the capital city to complain to the authorities about his bigamous union with Margarida. That was why Father Paulo had phoned him concerning his marriage papers, Romeu reasoned. He took a few steps backwards and almost tripped over the altar steps. He shouted, and his apprehensive voice echoed through the enclosed wilderness of the chapel, "What are you doing here? What do you want from me?"

António did not answer. When he reached the front pew, he offered his arm to the woman dressed in black, without taking his eyes off his father. The woman got up from her knees, slipped her arm into her son's, and together they approached the altar, closing in on Romeu.

"Who the devil is she?" Romeu shouted again, narrowing his eyes.

The woman in black wore very high heels and a tight, clinging dress. When she got nearer Romeu, she lifted her veil and revealed a heavily made-up face with bright red lips and thick false eyelashes. Romeu did not recognise her. She moved two steps nearer, pouted at him, her eyes hardened by a well-rehearsed promise of erotic delight, like a whore touting herself.

"Good God! Not you!" Romeu exclaimed in utter horror.

"We've come to give you a wedding present. Albeit a belated one, Father," said António.

Mother and son smiled at each other smugly.

"So, you've come all this way to tell Father Paulo of my marriage to your mother! It is a useless trick, my son, because I am properly and legally married to Margarida now."

"No, Father," said António. "We haven't come all this way to tell on you. We have a better plan in mind."

Romeu looked at his son and then his wife, trying to read their expressionless faces. He felt uncomfortable as they paced around him in a leisurely fashion. He said, "Father Paulo will be here any minute now. Tell me what you want and get out of here, before the Father and I throw you out."

Mother and son smiled at each other again. "Father Paulo won't be here," retorted António. "Nobody will be here. The Father never phoned you to meet him. It was I who rang and lured you here!"

"What?" Romeu uttered, dumbfounded and ashamed at having been fooled so easily.

"You heard me! Father Paulo is away, giving the last rites to a dying man. We fixed it all. We rang Father Paulo and pretended that he was needed at the hospital to administer the last rites to a dying man who had had a car accident. He won't be back for a while. And his assistant is away, too. There is nobody here. Just you and us," laughed António.

Romeu scanned the chapel for a way to escape.

"No, Father. It is of no use. I've locked up the church. You can't run away from us now. So we might as well have a cosy chat!"

"What do you want from me? Is it money?"

"Money?" Mother and son giggled. "No, Father. We want your life!"

"You can't be serious... you are joking..." Romeu stammered.

"We are serious all right," retorted his son.

Violeta extracted a kitchen knife from her black leather handbag, and twisted it in a provocative manner. "You won't get away with this murder," Romeu entreated, shocked by Violeta's physical as well as emotional transformation. She looked poised and self-assured now. But then Romeu had never known her or even bothered to know her. He had always taken her for granted.

"Fancy you talking about getting away with things," Violeta snapped at him. "You thought you could walk out on us and make bastards of my sons, just like that," she clicked her fingers, "and you got off scot-free, didn't you? You forget that in our community, we cherish our honour. We will get away with this murder, Romeu, because *you* dishonoured your family. Knowing that we killed you to avenge our honour, the Chinese back home will give us an alibi and will not collaborate with police investigations into the murder. We have driven all this way, Romeu, with your uncle's blessing. The Portuguese law by which you dismissed our marriage certificate won't save you now, will it?" Violeta said sarcastically.

"But why murder me in God's house?"

"You dirty rat!" Violeta shouted. "You became a Catholic to gain respectability for your marriage. You married Margarida in the cathedral here in Lourenço Marques. So why not die in God's house?" And with disdain, she added, "You said you wanted a wife who is a whore in bed, like Margarida. Well, Romeu, I've dressed up like a whore today to kiss you farewell." She embraced him and pressed her hideously bright lips against his, and before he could react, she plunged the knife into his body and stabbed him repeatedly, hissing, "Sixteen stabs – one for each year I've wasted on you, you rat!"

Romeu whined and mumbled in pain, and tried to pull himself away from her knife thrusts. He stumbled and fell. His blood-spattered body tumbled down the steps of the altar, and blood gushed all over the alabaster floor. Violeta sat astride the fallen body and stabbed it again and again, shrieking, "You rat, you cheat, you bastard," as if Romeu's flesh were meat that had to be tenderised by repeated beating. Violeta's son tore his father's trousers and underpants off, cut off his testicles, and threw them across the pews. He spat at the corpse four times, three on behalf of his brothers. Violeta wrapped the bloodstained knife in a white towel she had brought and hid them inside a black plastic bag. She wiped the lipstick off her lips and covered her face with the black veil. Arm-in-arm, mother and son walked out of the church.

The grounds surrounding it were deserted. They reached the main road and mingled unnoticed with the passers-by. Violeta felt light, happy, liberated. Her face regained.

DANGEROUS GAMES

Mei Lin strolled down India Street with her three children to buy ice cream cones at the café opposite the Praça do Município. India Street was in a bustling upmarket commercial quarter of the town centre, and it was known by that name because the shops there were mainly run by Indians. Drapers' shops and shoe shops were dotted along practically the whole length of the thoroughfare, its monotonous character only broken by a jeweller's located right in the middle section of it.

Mei Lin slowed down as she neared the jeweller's. The children ran ahead. She turned round and cast a glance back at the far end of the street, where her family's wholesale store, a large, two-storey grey building, stood at the junction of Azores Street and India Street, to check that no-one was watching her. She paused by the shop's display window and pretended to survey the glittering exhibits with interest. She lingered for a few seconds, just long enough to establish her presence and be seen by Saleem, the young owner of the shop. Then, she ambled on with languid steps, and when she passed the entrance door to the wide-fronted shop, Saleem had already planted himself there. He was wearing loose khaki shorts and standing on one leg, his body tilted and leaning against the doorpost. His other leg was folded, and the foot tucked in at the knee-bend of the standing leg, as if he were doing some yoga exercise. His well-manicured toes spread out like a semi-open fan in his flip-flops. As their eyes met, Mei Lin and Saleem nodded at each other as usual and exchanged their customary greeting, "Good afternoon." But today, Saleem detected more than her usual politeness in the way she had looked at him intensely and with feeling. An invitation, he sensed, for him to follow her.

Saleem hurried to the kitchen at the back of the shop, where his mother squatted on the concrete floor over a stone grinding-wheel, preparing flour. Lying through his teeth, Saleem said, "Please, Mother, come quickly to the shop! Something urgent cropped up and I have to go out. I'll be back in no time."

"What could be that urgent?" his mother asked, without interrupting her task.

"I'll explain when I get back. But hurry now, please!"

The woman brushed her hands several times to shake the flour off, wiped them on a moist cloth, and heaved her enormous body off the floor, panting. Then she staggered through to the shop.

Saleem and Mei Lin had never actually spoken to each other. The flirting and courtship had always been intimated from a distance. Mei Lin passed Saleem's shop every afternoon at three o'clock sharp, when Saleem would place himself at the doorway to see her.

They greeted each other with a coy smile and a nod, and although often enough Saleem's eyes had flashed out signals of desire for Mei Lin, neither had dared take the initiative of speaking to each other and become acquainted. Saleem knew she was a married woman with small children, and although he sensed she was unhappily married, and therefore potentially available and accessible, he also knew that he should abide by the implicit rule among his own narrow-minded community and that of Mei Lin's of not getting involved with a person of another race. Mei Lin had, up until now, evinced a polite interest in Saleem, but had never returned the body language he had often employed to draw her attention to his feelings for her. But today, her round, languid body movements exuded sensuality and insinuated at sexual longing. She jerked her head forward, gently but firmly, commanding him to follow her. Then she walked away with an exaggerated swaying of her hips. Saleem followed at some distance.

Senhor António's café was packed full. Saleem's eyes glanced over the sea of faces in search of Mei Lin, and lit up when he spotted her. He cruised through the tables in her direction. There, by the corner of the room, where a waist-high freezer was tucked away, stood Mei Lin, being served by a black waiter clad in a white cotton uniform. The children skirted around the freezer, pointing at the large tubs containing their favourite ice cream. While they watched expectantly the waiter scoop different flavours and piled colourful balls into crispy wafer cones, Mei Lai disengaged herself from their company and glided quietly to the cake counter where Saleem now lingered, surveying the cakes with the zeal of someone who intended purchasing a good many. Mei Lin also pretended to look at the cakes, and at the precise moment when she deliberately brushed her shoulder against Saleem's bare arm, she said without taking her eyes off the cakes, "Please meet me on Sunday at four o'clock, at the car park opposite where the Chinese marquee has been erected for the City Festival. Don't stay too close, but watch and follow me wherever I go." To Saleem's amazement, she squeezed his hand with affection, as she pleaded, "Please, do come." A whiff of sexuality blew past Saleem's nostrils, and as he inhaled the heady perfume she had so liberally splashed on herself for his benefit that afternoon, he felt his whole body aroused and quivering in anticipation.

*　　*　　*

Mei Lin was born in Hong Kong, and had reluctantly come to live in Beira as a result of her marriage to João, a Chinese Mozambican and only son of a prosperous merchant. She met him in Hong Kong when he became a student at the school she had attended since she was a child. They were both in their mid-teens and enjoyed playing badminton. Sharing similar interests, and more importantly, similar merchant-class backgrounds, they soon fell madly in love with each other. João's parents were elated when the young lovers declared their intention of getting married immediately after completing their secondary education. For they were snobs who, in spite of, or perhaps because of their humble beginnings, had set out to marry their son to someone from outside Mozambique. They were prejudiced against the local Chinese girls, whom they judged to lack in social graces and deportment. Mei Lin was beautiful, socially graceful, and brilliant at school. Her brothers were university graduates, and one of them was a practising doctor in Canada. She had all the right credentials for João's family's requirements. But if the latter were honest, they would admit that having a daughter-in-law from another country, and therefore family connections abroad, was an insurance against future insecurity. For João's parents were two of those Chinese Mozambicans who always looked upon their own country as outsiders, even though they were born in Mozambique themselves, and belonged to the second generation of Chinese immigrants. They had no confidence in the political stability of the African continent as a whole, and chose not to own any property in Mozambique, in the belief that it would be much easier for one to uproot oneself from a country if one didn't have any property there. Instead, they invested all their newly-found wealth outside the country, so that they could buy a place elsewhere if Mozambique ever became independent under Black African rule. This was the main reason why they had packed their son off to Hong Kong as a student, with the ambition that in due course he would find a suitable wife there. The fact that Hong Kong was a British colony and had to be returned to China one day, did not worry them. For China was not a country run by Blacks, they reasoned.

When Mei Lin and João got married, they dutifully returned to Beira, where João helped his father run the family's many business enterprises, as was customary for the first-born sons to do in Chinese families; and in João's case, the only son and heir to the family's wealth.

Like most Chinese women, Mei Lin gave birth to three children within the first four years of her marriage. The children, two boys and a girl, were as healthy and well-fed as money could buy, and the proud grandparents doted on them. But abundance of money also brought Mei Lin great unhappiness, for it bought her husband costly pleasures outside their family life. Back in Africa, and in the company of childhood friends, João began frequenting brothels and gambling joints. A vice, Mei Lin noted as she looked around her, against which few young men resisted, or wanted to resist.

After the birth of their third child, João practically spent the whole night out, returning home only in the morning at the hour the family's wholesale store opened for trading. When Mei Lin took him to task for neglecting her and the children, and squandering money at the Casino and whorehouses, he simply said, "Nag, nag! You wives always nag. It's a good thing I seldom sleep at home!" And when Mei Lin confided in her mother-in-law, with whom she got on well, and complained about her husband's infidelities, the old woman said light-heartedly, "But, my dear, you don't expect a man to be faithful to one woman only, do you? Men enjoy variety; they don't like eating the same dish every day. To tell you the truth, my own husband, your father-in-law, often goes to the same brothels as my son. When father and son run into each other there, they merely pat each other on the back and say: 'You here, too?' Mei Lin, you mustn't fret over my son's extra-marital activities. Or his gambling. Why don't you just enjoy yourself and travel like me, and be grateful for the relative independence that both you and I have because of our economic position? When I go to Rome and sit on one of those ancient stones at that old monument – what's it called, the Acropolis? – I feel contented and fulfilled. I don't want to worry about my husband's affairs. Men have affairs. So, be happy, Mei Lin, enjoy life as best as you can, and stop worrying about my son!"

Over the years, Mei Lin looked in vain for a weapon with which to strike and wound her husband once and for all. And now at last, that weapon was at hand. She would wield it and hurt João where he would never forget – in his macho pride. She had at first been repelled by Saleem's lusting over her, but she had gradually come to regard it as the most effective weapon she could exploit in order to humiliate João.

*   *   *

At the unpaved car park, a hundred yards equidistant from the National Cinema and the site where numerous marquees had been erected for the City Festival celebrations, Mei Lin excused herself from going directly to the fair with her husband, children, and parents-in-law, with the explanation that she needed to use the ladies' room at the cinema. She would, she said, join the family at the Chinese marquee where, together with other volunteers, she would be selling savouries at the food stalls. On hearing this, the little girl clutched her mother's hand and whimpered, "I want to go with you, Mummy." But Mei Lin sweetly but firmly nudged her towards Grandma, and repeated that they should not wait for her, but make directly for the fair.

And with a wave to the children, she turned abruptly on her red patent high-heeled shoes and walked away in the opposite direction. The child, hand-in-hand with Grandma, turned her head around every few steps to watch her mother disappear in the distance. It was as if she sensed that a big bad wolf was following her mother.

Not many cars away from where Mei Lin's husband had parked his Volvo, Saleem sat waiting in his own steel-domed vehicle. His avid eyes devoured every move Mei Lin made, and when she parted company with the family, he opened the door of his small beige Volkswagen, slithered lightly out into the tepid, hazy sun, and followed her.

A small queue of matinée-goers formed near the ticket office on the concrete pavement outside the cinema. As Mei Lin swayed past it, she heard wolf-whistling and "my China doll" calls directed at her. She ignored them, and raising her nose and chin high, proceeded straight into the cinema building. A sprinkling of people hung around in the foyer, but the tearoom was almost filled to capacity. The rich aroma of strong coffee permeated the drone of chatter, punctuated by the tinkling of crockery. Mei Lin paused at the steps leading to the tearoom, climbed a few steps, hesitated, then climbed down again. Without seeming to be looking for anyone in particular, and unsure of her destination, she made falteringly for the ladies' room on the same floor.

The ladies' room was small, but had all the basic essentials. It had a large, full-length mirror by the entrance door, and opposite it, a row of white enamel hand-basins. The toilets were but two tiny cubicles, nestled along one wall between the mirror and the hand-basins. Mei Lin went into the toilet that was free and closed the door. She was about to lock it, when it burst open and in squeezed Saleem. Mei Lin gasped in horror and said, "What are you doing here?" "What am I doing here?" Saleem answered. "Didn't you say I should follow you wherever you went?" He grabbed her by the wrists and pushed her against the tiled wall. "Let go of me," protested Mei Lin, trying to twist herself free of Saleem's tight grip. He began to kiss her; Mei Lin pursed her lips and swung her head from side to side so that Saleem couldn't get to her mouth. He lifted her skirt, and his sweaty hands groped her thighs. He pulled down her underpants and parted her legs, then he unzipped his cotton trousers, which flopped onto the stone floor, and thrust the full weight of his body against hers, jerking forward and backward countless times. Mei Lin felt disgusted with herself. Although she had not envisaged the possibility of being date-raped when she asked Saleem to meet her, she was now ashamed at the silent violence of her own unhappiness which had driven her to use Saleem. And she was doubly ashamed that she could not now complain about the actual outcome of events. She regretted she had unwittingly given Saleem the impression that she wanted to be seduced within the four walls of a cubicle where people went to shit and pee. And worse still, Mei Lin thought, he probably believed she was enjoying it. Exactly what she had expected from a rendezvous with a semi-stranger like Saleem, Mei Lin was not sure. In fact, she had never quite defined her expectations from the outset. Had she planned something as harmless as being seen to have tea with a man of another race? Or something bolder, suggestive of an affair, like being seen holding hands with a man other than her husband? Mei Lin knew she had only one objective: to hurt and humiliate her husband. And now, she found herself hurt and humiliated.

Saleem's gravelly groans grew louder and louder, hammering against her throbbing skull. Tears of humiliation flooded Mei Lin's livid face. Gathering all the strength she had left, she brought her right knee up as hard as she could in his groin. Taken by surprise, Saleem withdrew, clasped his arms, and let out a squeal of pain, his eyes half-shut and his moist, swollen penis still erect. Before Mei Lin could unlock the door and get out of the cubicle, she heard loud banging on the door and an angry male voice shout, "You there, come out at once! This is a respectable place. Have you no shame? Go and find some other place to do your fornicating!" It was the cinema manager, who had been alerted to the goings-on in the ladies' room by a woman who had been using the other toilet before Mei Lin got trapped. A crowd assembled outside. For news travelled fast in this small town, and twice as fast when it was saucy. A man and a woman caught having sex in a cinema toilet was a piece of news unheard of before, so people flocked in droves to see for themselves the reaction of the shamed lovers.

Mei Lin emerged expressionless from the ladies' room, and although she felt faint with embarrassment, she held her head high as she walked out of the building. She heard the manager shout, "You son-of-bitch, couldn't you have looked for a better place to fuck?" as he gave Saleem a kick in the backside. The spectators jeered and whistled. With her insides knotted and tense, Mei Lin stumbled back to the family Volvo in the car park.

In the safety of the car, Mei Lin sat tight in the back seat, but before she could take ten deep breaths, the door at her side was torn open and her angry husband shoved her to the far end of the seat. "You slut!" he said with disdain, and slapped her repeatedly, and punched her hard in one eye. Then he forced her out of the car and dragged her to the grounds where the fair was being held, Mei Lin's high heels slipping off several times. The mob crowded in on the unhappy couple, and pursued them until they reached the Chinese marquee. Outside the marquee, a frightened Saleem, who had immediately been seized by a gang of young Chinese men as he left the cinema, stood helpless in the middle of a human circle, awaiting his sentence.

"You, *monhé*," shouted João. "You raped my wife! And you think you can just walk away unpunished?"

"No," pleaded Saleem, "I did not rape your wife." And he went on to explain, "She asked me to meet her—"

"You liar!" João interrupted Saleem. But in the dark recesses of his mind, there lurked the suspicion that Saleem might be telling the truth, and he sensed, with shame, that the crowds did not altogether disbelieve Saleem's words. God, what a dishonour to my family –

my wife cuckolding me in a public lavatory, he said to himself. And with a man of another race! It was, however, inconceivable for him to admit such a possibility in public, so he grabbed Saleem by the collar, punched him and kicked him in the crotch, bellowing, "You liar, you liar!"

The young Chinese men who had formed a ring around Saleem, surged forward and each took turns to punch and kick him, as a gesture of loyalty and solidarity with one of their own. It was irrelevant whether Saleem was guilty or not guilty of raping Mei Lin. Theirs was a warning to any non-Chinese men not to mess around with their womenfolk. Saleem bled and writhed in pain on the grass. The crowds looked on.

"Stop it! Stop beating him!" Mei Lin shouted to the young men, and began to explain, "I did ask him to meet me today... It was not entirely his fault..."

"Shut up, you slut!" Her husband slapped her on the face. "Do you have no shame, woman?"

Young Indian men who were scattered among the crowds and witnessing one of their own being beaten up and so outnumbered, gathered together and plunged into the arena to take Saleem's side. Chinese and Indians punched and kicked one another in a display of equal brutality.

The police eventually arrived, blowing their whistles and baton charging at random in order to break up the fight.

"Let them fight it out," chanted some spectators.

"You shouldn't interfere," others exclaimed. "It's a private matter of honour between the *chinas* and the *monhés*!"

"Yes, yes!" The crowd cheered.

Then some smart aleck in the crowd shouted, "As long as it's the *chinas* versus the *monhés*, and not them together against us Portuguese, let them fight!" And the spectators clapped and laughed.

The police officer blew his whistle to quieten the crowds and said, "Quiet, all of you! We are all Portuguese here – whether you are Chinese, Indian, Black, or White."

"That's a good one," shouted a confident Chinese man. "We're only Portuguese when you want us to pay taxes, or when you want our sons to go and fight in the war!" And the crowds laughed in good humour.

"Now break it up, break it up!" the policeman ordered, dispersing the crowds.

* * *

After the rape incident, Mei Lin's life continued as usual, ensconced in routine and family rituals. Although the relationship between her and João had become non-existent, they remained as husband and wife. And in the rare moments they found themselves together alone, silence was their mutual companion. Often, she passed Saleem's shop, and on such occasions, Saleem's mother would emerge from the shop and chase her away down the street with a broom, calling her names and shouting, "Fancy seducing my son and then having him accused of rape. Go away! Don't come back this way."

Many a time, Saleem had longed for an opportunity to speak with Mei Lin, and she with him. He wanted to apologise for having raped her, and she to say how sorry she was for the way he had been beaten up. Strangely, a peculiar bond of empathy and tenderness developed between them in spite of the violence in which they had been caught. Her unhappiness and vulnerability were crystal clear now, and she had become utterly solitary, for even though people of her own race were not treating her as a disgraceful, fallen woman to her face, she was aware they scoffed at her behind her back. Once or twice, Mei Lin's and Saleem's paths crossed in the vegetable market in the town centre, and although they wished to speak to each other then, they didn't dare, in the full glare of a watchful public. Words thus remained unsaid and, with the passage of time, died in hearts which no longer had the energy to make the extra effort of seeking to communicate. The years plodded on and, one morning, the bomb of history exploded. And the cotton-swaddled little world they had known up until then was shattered...

...And in the white panic of the winter of 1975, when settlers queued up at travel agents to purchase tickets to leave the country for good, Mei Lin ran into Saleem. Looking relaxed, and at peace with herself, she took the initiative of approaching him, and spoke to him as if they had been friends for a long time. "I see you are leaving, too. I'm going to Canada with my daughter, to join my brother. He lives there."

"But aren't you going back to Hong Kong with your family?" Saleem asked, surprised.

"No," Mei Lin answered without hesitation. "João and I are splitting up. He is going to Hong Kong with his parents and our two sons." After a pause, she added, "You know, for the first time in these long unhappy years, I feel confident about myself. I'm no longer afraid. And I have to thank Independence for that. Had Independence not come, I wouldn't have bothered to make a choice as to where I want to go and with whom I don't want to share my life any more. I would just have stayed put with João here in Beira and gone on living my complacent little existence. I am sorry, Saleem, for what happened on that day at the fair."

"So am I, Mei Lin. If only you knew how much..."

"Yes, I know." And she reassured him with a tilt of her head and a gentle smile. Then she asked, "And where are you going? Back to India?"

"Yes, I *was* going back to India," Saleem said. "But on second thoughts, I think I could try my luck in Canada. Do you think I could?" Saleem asked, hopefully.

Mei Lin looked deeply into his eyes and, smiling, said, "Why not? Canada is as good as any place for one to start one's life all over again."

SMALL MERCIES

Eva was helping her parents in their eating house in Chinatown, as she always did after school hours, when the telephone rang. Her father dragged his flip-flops to the table where the telephone was, picked up the receiver slowly, and drawled, "Hello, Mr Wong's eating house... Yes, just a moment." Covering the mouth of the receiver with his rough hand, he called out, "Eva, it's for you, from the *Notícias da Beira*." "For me?" Eva exclaimed, blushing. She was surprised, nervous, and expectant. For she had written a short story, "When the Police Knock on the Door", and sent it to the local newspaper for them to consider publishing. A phone call, she hoped, could only mean good news. She finished pouring the tea into tin mugs for the African customers she was serving, put down the huge aluminium teapot on an unoccupied table, and picked her way gingerly to the other end of the room to receive the call.

Eva was eighteen years old and about to complete her final year of secondary education that November. She hoped to go to university, but whether her wishes would eventually materialise or not depended very much on the generosity and goodwill of Mr Chin. But above all, on his whim. For Mr Chin, a wealthy merchant impressed by Eva's academic performance at school and her enthusiasm for a university education, had repeatedly intimated that he was willing to finance her university studies abroad. In Europe. Rich people with a conscience, Eva reckoned, whose own children were low-performers at school and thus unable to gain entry to university, projected the aspirations they held for their own flesh and blood onto less fortunate children, deigning to help them by becoming their social godparents. Often, they practised these acts of charity for their own vanity and status, for they enjoyed being looked upon as benefactors. But, Eva reasoned, in a society where education was not a right but a privilege, one willingly accepted the rare gift of a scholarship in whatever wrapping it was given. Condescension, Eva thought, was the donor's problem, not the recipient's. Besides, Mr Chin had said that his gift had no strings attached. And had her parents not made enough sacrifices so that she could go to university? She was, after all, the only one in her family to have had the benefit of a private secondary education. That was because she was the youngest of the children, and by the time she reached the age of eleven, her parents felt they could afford the monthly school fees. Or rather, could just about afford them. Eva recollected with a tinge of shame how she always paid her school fees on the last day of the month instead of the first, as her colleagues did. Her class tutor, not wishing to embarrass her more, merely said "thank you" without looking at her.

"Yes... Yes... Yes... Yes..." was all that Eva could mutter over the phone. She was flushed with joy and excitement. She dashed to her parents, swallowed deeply, and said, almost gasping, "They are going to publish the story I wrote in next Sunday's edition, on their literary page. They've also asked me to go and have a chat with them at the office. They are offering me a traineeship with the newspaper when I've completed my exams. I can't believe my luck!" Eva groped for her stool and sat down.

"That is wonderful news, daughter! But you want to go to university, don't you?" her mother asked. Her father nodded in agreement with the spirit of his wife's question.

"Of course I do, Mother. But don't you see what this means? I now have two options – to go to university and do a degree in literature, or take up a traineeship with the *Notícias da Beira*. It means I don't have to depend on Mr Chin's patronage alone. If, by some whim, he decided not to fulfil his promise, I now have the option of getting a job where my skills with words are used. And one day, when I've earned enough, I can become a student and pay for my own university education. I have always wanted to work with words, as a writer or a journalist. But the exciting thing is that I can now make a choice. And freedom is about making choices and having more than one option. I am so excited, Mother and Father, I can't wait to tell the school my good news."

Mrs Wong wrapped her arms around her daughter and said, "Yes, Eva, you have come quite a long way compared to your less fortunate sisters. I feel blessed for you, for the opportunities you are going to have..."

"Oh, Mother, they'll only be relative opportunities. I know I'll have a long struggle ahead of me, as a woman, and as a Chinese woman, seeking to earn a living in a man's world, a white man's world!"

"One day, when you have children of your own, Eva, I'm sure they'll have even better opportunities, and probably equal to those of their male counterparts, because by then our third generation here in this land will truly belong."

"I don't know about that, Mother. We may feel we belong here. But we only belong if we are accepted as belonging. I mean, people see what they want to see. We are, of course, Portuguese on paper, but we are as Portuguese as the whites and others wish to see us. More likely than not, Chinese of whatever generation will always be regarded as Chinese, not truly natives of this land. Both blacks and whites look at us and say straightaway, 'You are not like us. You have a yellow skin and slant eyes. You are Chinese.' We just can't win. The problem is with them, in the same way that the privilege of considering us as Portuguese or not is with them."

"You are probably right," said her mother.

"Of course she is right," her father remarked.

"Whatever the future brings, today I feel good about myself. Let's celebrate the good news by closing our eating house for the rest of the day."

"Yes, let's do that," her parents agreed. And that day, Eva and her parents gave free rein to their imagination over her many prospects and her good fortune.

Eva, being the youngest of seven children – four girls and three boys – had enjoyed more security, comforts, and education than any of her brothers and sisters. Because of this, she had few fond memories of sister number three's attitude towards her. She remembered vividly the afternoon she obtained her Fifth-Grade examination results. She had passed with flying colours and was therefore not required to do the oral examination. Her father was so proud of her performance that he announced to the family that Eva would stay on at school and do her Seventh Grade, even though that meant more sacrifices for the parents. Who knows? he went on to say, should their circumstances improve, Eva might even go to university. On hearing this, Eva's third sister, five years her senior, burst into floods of sour tears. She wailed over the lack of opportunities for education that she and her brothers and sisters had suffered, as none of them had more than a bilingual primary education at the local Chinese School, except for lucky brother number two. Having won some money on a lottery, he journeyed to Southern Rhodesia for a short spell, where he learnt and obtained a good enough command of English to secure a job as an office clerk with a British firm based in Beira. But Eva, sister number three scowled, why should Eva go on studying in a private school and then go to university, when she herself had to slave away in her parents' eating house for no proper wages at all? Why shouldn't Eva, who had the good fortune of completing her Fifth Grade, now work in the parents' shop just as she had to? And with each tearful sob, she worked up her resentment against Eva into a higher and higher pitch, until she exploded into an uncontrollable rage and fled to the kitchen to fetch a cleaver. She returned to the room where the family was gathered and aimed the cleaver at Eva, slicing the air as her sister ducked from her blows. The parents wrestled with her and tried to wrench the sharp weapon from her, but she held on tightly to the wooden handle. Then, unexpectedly, almost to spite her parents, she dropped the cleaver. As her father's Neanderthal-shaped foot was digging firmly into the floor at a right angle to the cleaver's shiny blade, the latter fell onto his big toe and chopped it off. It rolled over and swayed limply on the lino floor in a tiny fountain of blood.

Sister number three remained unrepentant of her behaviour. To further make her point, she no longer worked at her parents' eating house after Eva's school hours. Eva, she argued, should give a hand then, and to hell with her school homework! Hadn't she had enough privileges compared with everyone else in the family? And so Eva began working in her parents' eating house when she finished school.

Of her two other sisters, Eva had only vague recollections, because of the age gap which separated them. By the time she started primary school, her eldest sister had already been married off to some older man in Malawi. Eva remembered eavesdropping on a conversation between her parents and a visiting aunt, and learning that her brother-in-law had already got a wife back in Hong Kong, and that although her own parents were aware of this, they turned a blind eye to his bigamy and pretended not to know it. With her eldest sister married off, there was one less mouth to feed, Eva heard her parents explain to her aunt. So, from an early age, she began to learn that poverty always demanded painful sacrifices from the older children. In later years, she heard friends casually mention that her sister, who ran a take-away in Malawi, was often seen weeping over a wok while she stir-fried, with her right hand, customers' orders and balanced her baby on her left hip. Now that Eva was eighteen, her sister and family were immigrants in the United States, and ran an ice-cream shop in San Francisco.

Of sister number two, Eva remembered only slightly more. The thing that stuck in her mind about sister number two was the speculation her rejection of a marriage proposal from a well-to-do trader in the capital city had generated among her peers. And amid gasps of horror, the shocked community saw sister number two marry instead a penniless oyster seller who, over the years, became known as "that cheat of an oyster seller". On his daily rounds to customers' shops and houses, he lugged a large bucket of oysters made out of an old tin drum, and sold oysters by the mugful. He cheated his customers unashamedly by measuring the oysters in a mug with a false bottom made from a tin disc. "Why do you cheat your own race with a mug like that?" his Chinese customers reprimanded him, but went on buying from him nevertheless. "We can understand you playing that sort of trick on the Portuguese," they said, "but on your own people... really!" But the oyster seller only chuckled, never bothering to deny the accusations, as it was patently obvious that he had tampered with the mug and was indeed cheating.

Sister number two, Eva grew up to learn, had turned down a good marriage proposal because she was no longer a virgin at the time, and was too afraid to marry into a well-to-do family with good connections, and be found out and put to shame. She chose instead a poor husband with no family to answer to. How and to whom she had lost her virginity, Eva never probed further, for her parents seldom referred to sister number two, preferring instead to disown her as a member of the family, except on Chinese New Year Day, when she and her husband joined in the family celebrations.

Of her brothers, Eva had no reason to complain, as they were too busy earning their own living to resent her academic inclinations and achievements. Her eldest brother ran a bar, just around the corner from her parents' eating house, where drunken customers smashed up more glasses and empty bottles than bought drinks. And brother number three, her senior only by four years, had been conscripted and was now serving as a cook in the army. Brother number two was too happy with his job as a clerk to envy her exam performance at school.

When business was slack in their eating house, Eva would draw up a stool by her mother's side at the counter and teach her how to read and write in Portuguese, for her mother was illiterate in the language. Then, standing behind her mother and leaning over her shoulder, Eva held her mother's stiff, work-calloused right hand with her own, and guided it in slow movements, producing hesitant but coherent letters on paper. Often, her mother grumbled she was too old to learn to read and write in a new language, but on such occasions, Eva insisted firmly that the only way she could read the stories her daughter would write and have published one day would be to persevere in her efforts. Mother and daughter buried their heads together and worked doubly hard on reading and writing, oblivious to the newly arrived African customers who would bang on the counter demanding to be served immediately, chanted "jeeng-gau-aah, jeeng-gau-aah", making fun of the Chinese language, and shouted abuse at the two women, vowing to take them when the country was black once again. Obscene insults of the kind she had to tolerate from customers in her parents' eating house strengthened Eva's determination to break free from the expectations the average Chinese had of earning a living by shopkeeping.

At school, Eva acquired a great love for literature, and her own instincts challenged her into channelling basic ingredients, such as her own poverty, grievances, fears, and hopes, into some artistic endeavour. She began writing short stories in exercise books, poignant stories which cried out against her oppressive surroundings and snapped at her humdrum existence. Stories for which she received commendations at school and a prize for literature at the end of the year.

Then, one day, in response to a biased article in the local newspaper, which sweepingly portrayed the

Chinese as a race of inveterate law-breakers, trading after licensed hours, Eva wrote a short story of protest against odious stereotyping of her race and sent it to the newspaper. In her story, she presented Chinese people from various walks of life, and gave them qualities that were universal and human. She explained why many small shopkeepers, who catered solely for Blacks in areas such as Chipangara, Munhava, and Manga, traded outside licensed hours, risking having police patrols knocking on their doors and paying fines. Poverty, Eva pointed out, and the underlying desire of every Chinaman to be self-sufficient by working hard and keeping his shop open during long, unsocial hours, impelled him to trade later than licensed. On the other hand, Eva reminded her readers, shopkeepers who catered for a white settler market traded within the licensed hours and never broke the law. To suggest, as the article in the paper had done, that the Chinese as a people suffered from an endemic disease of law-breaking, was insensitive, unintelligent, and absurd, Eva argued. What the newspaper needed to consider was the social background of Chinese traders and include, among all Chinese, the many successful professionals who didn't have to submit to the indignities of harassment, either from the police or their customers.

And now, to her surprise, the newspaper was not only going to publish her story, but was also offering her a traineeship. Such generosity from the owners of the newspaper, Eva wondered, was perhaps a publicity stunt. A way of showing the public that, irrespective of the colour of one's skin, or who knows, perhaps because of it, if one had a special talent, one could and was given a chance to prove it, as a gesture of goodwill from those in authority. Hadn't she often heard well-intentioned whites preach positive discrimination in favour of non-whites? Well, Eva mused, whatever the reason behind the newspaper's offer of a traineeship, she felt she was now on the threshold of freedom.

She was intelligent and perceptive, and understood that freedom was only relative. But for the present, all that mattered was that she felt free from the constraints of her own poverty. She had two options to choose from, and that was a start; the beginning of a new era. She thanked lady luck for such small mercies. One day, she would question the nature and degree of her newfound freedom, and perhaps the illusion of that freedom she now sensed in her grasp would evaporate. How free she would be, as a journalist, from censorship, whether from her employer or the political authorities, were serious issues she would face in due course. For the present, she wished only to savour the sweet taste of freedom she now believed she enjoyed. Tomorrow was another day. And freedom is as relative and transient as the force of circumstances.

GLOSSARY

Bacalhau de creme – salt cod baked in a creamy sauce.

Batuque – an African drum dance.

Bolos de arroz – Portuguese muffins made partly with rice flour.

Cacimbo – a morning or evening mist.

Capulana – a printed cotton gown worn by women.

China – a derogatory term for a Chinese person.

Escudo – currency used in colonial Mozambique.

FRELIMO – acronym for the Mozambican independence movement, *Frente de Libertação de Moçambique.*

Machamba – a small farm or plantation.

Machambeiro – the owner of a *machamba.*

Mainato – a male domestic servant.

Muzungo – boss or master.

Monhé – a derogatory term for an Indian.

Mulata – a woman of mixed African and European background.

Pastéis de nata – Portuguese custard tarts.

Piri-piri – a spicy sauce or marinade used on grilled chicken, and popular in Mozambique.

Woo kok – a Chinese taro croquette.

ABOUT THE AUTHOR

Celeste Young was born and raised in Beira, Mozambique. She was educated there, in South Africa, and in the United Kingdom, where she has lived for over fifty years. She has a degree in Philosophy with Political Science from Queen's University Belfast, and a Diploma in Social Administration from the University of Bristol. She is a retired language teacher.